WIDOW

BOOK TWO OF THE VALENSI CHRONICLES

C.L. STEGALL

S TUDIO V ALENSI

TABLE OF CONTENTS:

PROLOGUE

THE HUNT

PRESENT DAY

CHARLOTTE, NIGHT

Ross moved through the warehouse district like a man with nothing left to lose.

Which, if he was being honest with himself, wasn't far from the truth.

The smell hit him first. Rust and river water and the faint chemical tang of whatever they manufactured in the squat buildings that lined Statesville Avenue. Late October had settled over Charlotte like a damp wool blanket, not quite cold enough for frost but enough to drive the homeless into shelters and clear the streets of anyone who didn't have business being out at two in the morning.

Ross had business.

He kept to the shadows between the streetlights, his boots finding the quiet spots on the cracked pavement without conscious thought. Muscle memory. The Army had drilled it into him years ago, and the years since had only sharpened the instinct. Move without sound. Watch without being seen. Hunt without becoming the hunted.

The Glock at his hip was a familiar weight, though he knew it would be useless if things went sideways. Steel didn't kill them. Steel just pissed them off.

The knife strapped to his thigh was another matter entirely.

Madronite blade, eight inches long, perfectly balanced. It had cost him three months of favors and a conversation with Matthew

DiBondra that still surfaced in his nightmares from time to time. The things that man knew. The things he'd seen. The things he'd built his entire empire around destroying.

But the knife worked. God help him, it worked.

He'd used it four times now. Four monsters turned to ash and memory. Four nights of shaking so hard afterward that he couldn't hold a cup of coffee until well past dawn. The crash always came. It was the price of the high. That crystalline clarity that descended over him during the hunt, when everything else fell away and there were only the target and the mission and the purity of purpose.

Maladaptive coping, the VA therapist had called it, back when he'd still been going to sessions.

Ross called it the only thing keeping him upright.

Tonight would make five.

The intel had come through Temper three days ago. A pattern of disappearances in the NoDa arts district. Young men, late teens to early twenties, the kind who worked delivery jobs and walked home alone after their shifts ended. Two had turned up dead in alleys, throats torn out, bodies drained of blood so thoroughly that the medical examiner had written it off as some new synthetic drug causing hemorrhaging.

The ME didn't know any better.

Ross did.

A third victim was still missing. Probably dead by now, dumped somewhere the cops wouldn't find him for weeks. Maybe months. The ones who fed for pleasure rather than necessity rarely bothered cleaning up after themselves. They wanted the bodies found. Wanted the fear. Wanted the newspapers speculating about serial killers and gang violence while they laughed in the shadows.

Hawthorn called them Baneful. Valensi who had abandoned whatever passed for conscience among their kind and embraced the predator within. They were rare. Most of the monsters kept to the old rules, fed without killing, maintained the secrecy that had protected them for millennia. But when one went rogue, the body count climbed fast.

Ross had spent the last two nights mapping her hunting ground, learning her patterns. She was young, as far as he could tell. Maybe a decade or two since her turning. The older ones were more careful, more controlled. They didn't leave bodies where humans could find them. This one was sloppy. Arrogant.

She thought she was invincible.

They all thought that. Right up until they weren't.

He spotted her at 2:17 AM.

She was standing in the mouth of an alley off Matheson Avenue, her body language loose and casual, like she was waiting for a bus that would never come. Pretty, in that way they all were. Dark hair, pale skin, features that belonged on a magazine cover. The predators always looked like angels. It seemed to be part of the design.

But Ross saw the way her head turned. Too smooth. Too precise. Tracking something down the block with the patience of a cat watching a mouse.

He followed her gaze and felt his stomach clench.

A kid.

Couldn't have been older than seventeen, maybe eighteen. Thin and gangly in the way teenage boys were before they grew into their frames. He was walking fast, head down, earbuds in, a thermal delivery bag slung over one shoulder. The logo on his jacket marked him as working for one of those late-night food apps. Probably trying to make a few extra bucks before school tomorrow.

Probably wouldn't make it home at all if Ross didn't move.

The woman, the thing, pushed off from the wall and began to follow. Her stride was unhurried, confident. She knew the kid couldn't outrun her. Knew that no one would hear him scream in this part of town at this hour. Knew that she had all the time in the world to play with her food.

Ross moved parallel, keeping to the shadows, his hand finding the knife at his thigh. The Glock would have been louder, would have drawn attention. The knife was silent.

The knife was final.

The kid turned down a side street. Bad choice. It dead-ended at a loading dock behind a shuttered furniture warehouse. The woman's pace quickened. She was done waiting.

Ross broke into a run.

He came around the corner just as she was reaching for the boy, her hand closing on his shoulder, spinning him around. The kid's eyes went wide. Not with fear, not yet. Just confusion. Pretty girl. Dark alley. His brain hadn't caught up to the danger.

"Hey," Ross called out. "Step away from him."

She turned. The confusion on the kid's face was nothing compared to the irritation on hers. Her features shifted in the darkness. Subtle, barely perceptible, but Ross had learned to see it. The way the shadows seemed to gather around her eyes. The way her lips pulled back just slightly, revealing teeth that were longer than they should have been.

"Walk away," she said. Her voice was honey and broken glass. "This doesn't concern you."

"Yeah." Ross drew the knife. "It really does."

Her eyes found the blade, and her expression shifted. Recognition. Fear, maybe, though she buried it quickly beneath contempt.

"You're one of them," she said. "Hawthorn's little attack dog."

"Woof."

She moved.

Fast. Faster than anything human had a right to be. One moment she was ten feet away, the next she was in his face, her hand closing around his throat with fingers like steel cables. The impact drove him backward into a stack of wooden pallets, the wood splintering against his spine.

The kid screamed.

Ross drove the knife toward her chest, but she caught his wrist, twisted. Bones ground against each other. He felt something give—not a break, not quite, but close. The knife clattered to the concrete.

"Stupid," she hissed, her face inches from his. Her breath was cold, smelling of copper and something older, darker. "Did you really think you could take me alone?"

Ross headbutted her.

It hurt him more than it hurt her. His vision went white for a moment, stars exploding behind his eyes. But it surprised her enough to loosen her grip. He dropped, rolled, came up with the knife back in his hand.

She was on him again before he could set his feet.

The next sixty seconds were chaos. Claws and fists and the blade singing through air that was suddenly thick with blood. Some of it his, more of it hers. She was stronger, faster, more experienced in the close-quarters violence that was her birthright. But Ross had spent six years learning how to kill in places where dying was the default setting, and he'd spent the years since learning how to kill things that shouldn't exist at all.

He took a hit to the ribs that cracked at least two of them. Another across his face that opened his cheek to the bone. He kept getting up. He always kept getting up. It was the only thing he knew how to do anymore.

The kid had pressed himself against the loading dock, frozen in terror. At some point during the fight, he'd tried to run. She'd backhanded him almost casually, sending him sprawling across the concrete, his head striking the corner of a rusted dumpster.

He wasn't moving.

Ross saw the blood pooling beneath the boy's skull. His hands stopped shaking. His breathing steadied. The chaos of the fight simplified into a single, clean purpose.

The woman saw the change in him. Saw it and, for the first time, looked uncertain.

"You—" she started.

Ross didn't let her finish.

He feinted left, drew her guard, then drove the Madronite blade up under her ribs at an angle that would have punctured a human heart. She wasn't human, but the blade didn't care about anatomy. The blade only cared about what it was made of.

She screamed.

It wasn't a human sound. It wasn't even close to human. It was the sound of something ancient and terrible realizing, far too late, that it was about to die.

The Madronite spread through her system like fire through dry kindling. Ross watched her face contort, pain, rage, disbelief, as her flesh began to crack from within, dark lines spreading across her skin like shattered porcelain. Her eyes found his, and for just a moment, he saw something almost human in them. Fear. Genuine, mortal fear.

Then she came apart.

The collapse took maybe thirty seconds, but it felt longer. Cells disintegrating, tissue dissolving, bones crumbling to powder. By the end there was nothing left but a pile of greasy ash and the faint smell of something burning.

Ross stood over the remains, chest heaving, blood streaming down his face. His hands were shaking. They always shook afterward. The high was already fading, leaving behind the familiar crash. The hollow emptiness where purpose used to be.

Five, he thought. Five monsters.

Then he remembered the boy.

Marcus was alive. Barely.

Ross knelt beside him, checking for a pulse, assessing the damage. The head wound was bad. Scalp lacerations always bled like hell, but this one had the ugly look of a fracture beneath it. The kid's eyes were open but unfocused, tracking nothing.

"Hey," Ross said, patting his cheek. "Hey, stay with me. Can you hear me?"

"The... the woman..." Marcus's voice was thin, distant. "Her face... her face..."

"I know. Don't think about that. Help is coming."

It was a lie. Ross hadn't called anyone. Hadn't had time. In the blink of an eye, he looked at the knife, knew he couldn't let the cops take it. He looked around and reached under the garbage bin and found a small space along the underside and slid the knife into it. No time left. He'd have to remember this place. Or, let Temper know.

As if summoned by the thought, the wail of sirens cut through the night. Not close yet, but approaching. Someone in the surrounding buildings must have heard the screaming. Or the gunfire. Had he used the Glock? He couldn't remember. Everything after drawing the knife was a blur of violence and instinct.

"Just stay still," he told Marcus. "The ambulance is coming. You're going to be okay."

Another lie. The kid had seen things tonight that would never be okay. Would never make sense. Would wake him up screaming for years to come, assuming the head trauma didn't take those memories away entirely.

Maybe that would be a mercy, Ross thought. Maybe forgetting is the kindest thing.

He heard tires squealing somewhere close. Doors slamming. Voices shouting. The cavalry, arriving too late as always.

Ross didn't run.

He could have. Part of him wanted to. The part that knew how this would look, knew what questions would be asked, knew that standing over a bleeding teenager next to a pile of ash that used to be a woman was not a situation that resolved itself easily.

But he couldn't leave Marcus. Not like this. Not broken and bleeding and staring at something his mind couldn't process.

"FREEZE! HANDS WHERE WE CAN SEE THEM!"

Ross raised his hands slowly. Blood, his and hers and some that he couldn't identify, dripped from his fingers onto the concrete.

"Step away! NOW!"

He simply did as he was told. No resistance at all. Gave some distance between him and the boy.

"On your knees! Hands behind your head!"

He complied. The concrete was cold and wet beneath him, soaking through his jeans. He could see Marcus from this angle, could see the EMTs pushing past the cops to reach him, could see the confusion on their faces as they tried to make sense of the scene.

Good luck with that, he thought. I've been trying to make sense of it for years.

They cuffed him with his face pressed into the pavement. Someone was reading him his rights, but the words washed over him without registering. All he could focus on was the pile of ash a few feet away, already scattering in the light breeze. By morning there would be nothing left. No evidence. No body. Just a case file full of questions that would never be answered.

A cop crouched beside him, shining a flashlight in his face. Young guy, maybe mid-twenties, with the kind of fresh-scrubbed earnestness that suggested he hadn't been on the job long enough to get it beaten out of him.

"Jesus Christ," the cop muttered, taking in the wounds on Ross's face. "What the hell happened here?"

Ross laughed. It came out wrong. Too sharp, too hollow. The cop flinched.

"You wouldn't believe me if I told you."

They put him in the back of a cruiser while the EMTs worked on Marcus. He watched through the window as they loaded the kid onto a stretcher, his head wrapped in gauze, an IV already running into his arm. Alive. That was something. That had to count for something.

The cops were poking around the scene with flashlights, taking pictures, looking for evidence that would explain what had happened here. One of them crouched near the pile of ash, frowning, probably trying to figure out what the hell he was looking at. He'd never figure it out. None of them would. They'd write it up as industrial residue, or accelerant, or just leave it out of the report entirely.

Humans were remarkably good at not seeing what they didn't want to see.

Ross let his head fall back against the seat and closed his eyes. The shaking had gotten worse. It always got worse in the aftermath, once the adrenaline wore off and there was nothing left but the hollow place where purpose used to be.

Five monsters now. Five kills. Five nights of wondering if he was the hero of this story or just another kind of predator.

The faces came back to him, as they always did. The ones he'd killed. The ones he'd failed to save. Rufus, lying in a pool of blood on the floor outside the laboratory. The look in that Valensi's eyes right before she'd snapped his neck. The same casual disregard you'd show while swatting a fly.

We will see you end up as the cattle you are.

Ross opened his eyes. The first gray light of dawn was beginning to creep across the Charlotte skyline, painting the warehouses in shades of ash and bone.

He thought about Marcus. About the story the kid would tell. Or not tell, depending on how the head trauma shook out. About the way he'd looked at Ross at the end, not with gratitude but with a kind of numb horror. Like he couldn't tell the difference between the monster and the man who'd killed it.

Maybe there isn't one, Ross thought. Maybe that's the point.

The cruiser door opened. Someone was talking to him, asking questions he couldn't quite hear. He let himself be pulled from the car, let himself be led toward the station, let himself become another problem for the system to process.

Somewhere across Charlotte, in an office he'd never seen, a case file was being born. A file full of contradictions and impossibilities. A file that would land on someone's desk and refuse to make sense no matter how many times they read it.

Somewhere across Charlotte, a woman named Brianna Van Demir would inherit that file.

She had no idea what was coming.

Neither did Ross.

But as the sun crept higher and the night's horrors faded into the harsh light of morning, one thought crystallized in his fractured mind with perfect, terrible clarity:

This isn't over.

It was only beginning.

1

BEFORE DAWN

It had been forever since Brianna had flinched at the sight of the sun.

The first rays touched the horizon, and Brianna's skin remembered.

Not pain—not anymore. But her body still carried the memory of it. The way her hands had blistered and split that first deliberate morning in 1847, when she'd forced herself to stand in a shaft of sunlight for three seconds. Just three seconds. She'd screamed until her throat tore. Had healed in the darkness of a wine cellar, weeping, certain she'd made a terrible mistake.

She'd done it again the next week. Four seconds.

And again. And again. Century after century of deliberate exposure, of flesh blackening and splitting, of healing only to burn again. Most who knew what she was attempting had called her insane. The Magistrate herself had tried to forbid it. But Brianna had kept going—five seconds, ten, thirty, a minute, an hour—until the day she'd stood in full noon sun and felt nothing but warmth.

That had been sixty-three years ago. She still remembered the taste of her own tears. Joy and disbelief and something like grief for all the pain it had cost her.

Brianna Van Demir had reversed her destiny.

Standing on her front porch in the gray light before dawn, she drew in a deep breath and let it out slowly. The Carolina pines stood sentinel around her property, their needles whispering secrets to each other in the early morning breeze. Her breakfast was settling in her stomach. Eggs, toast, bacon, the kind of human food that her kind needed in abundance to fuel their accelerated metabolisms. And she sipped her coffee while the sky slowly brightened from charcoal to rose.

She eased into the rocking chair by the door and curled her bare feet beneath her. The wood creaked softly, a familiar rhythm. She'd sat in this chair a thousand mornings, watching the sun rise through these same trees, and she suspected she'd sit here a thousand more before this identity ran its course and she had to move on.

Move on. Such a simple phrase for such a complicated thing.

She started to hum, Cole Porter's "Let's Fall in Love," and let her mind drift in that dangerous space between memory and the present. Eight hundred and seventy years of memories. Nearly a millennium of identities built and abandoned, relationships begun and ended, homes made and left behind.

All those lifetimes of learning, over and over again, how to be alone.

The low greeting came from the edge of the porch, pulling her back to the present.

"Meow."

A gorgeous slate-gray cat leapt onto the railing with an ease that belied the six-foot distance from ground to wood. The Chartreux began cleaning her paws with the careful precision of a creature who knew exactly how good she looked and wanted to make absolutely certain everyone else knew it too.

"You preen like a peacock, old friend," Brianna said.

Mimi turned her brilliant amber eyes toward Brianna, and their minds connected in an instant. That peculiar bridge that had developed between them over decades of proximity and weekly blood-sharing.

"I look good, yes?" The thoughts were crystal clear, though still somewhat primitive even after all these years. Feline minds weren't built for complex language, but Mimi had come a long way from their first meeting in New York, back when she'd been a half-starved kitten scrounging in a Chelsea alley.

That had been sixty-three years ago. Mimi should have been dead five times over by now.

She wasn't.

"Of course you do, dear one," Brianna replied, speaking aloud while sending her thoughts along with the words. It felt less strange that way. Less like she was losing her mind, talking to a cat. "Who could ever argue otherwise? Good hunting?"

"Mice. Not bad." Mimi finished cleaning one paw and started on the other. "Got rabbit, too."

"Well done. Still hungry?"

"Yes."

Mimi completed her ablutions and leapt down from the railing, meandering toward the door with the proprietary air of a creature who knew she owned everything she surveyed. The small entrance flap that Brianna had installed when they'd moved here swung gently as the cat pushed through.

"You coming?" Mimi thought.

Brianna breathed out a short laugh and rose from her chair. She stretched. More habit than necessity; her body didn't stiffen the way human bodies did. And peered once more at the horizon. The sun was cresting now, spilling gold and amber across the pine tops, painting the world in colors that should have been fatal to her.

She never tired of seeing it. After a century of deliberately burning herself to build this tolerance, after decades more of learning to move through the daylight world like she belonged there, the sunrise had become a touchstone for her own humanity. A reminder that she had fought for this. Earned it. That she was not merely a creature of darkness, no matter what her nature demanded.

She finished her coffee and followed Mimi inside.

The kitchen was quiet save for the soft hum of the refrigerator and Mimi's patient breathing.

The cat sat upon her wooden bench beside her food bowl, tracking Brianna's movements with those ancient amber eyes. Waiting. Mimi had learned patience over six decades, though it still wasn't her strongest virtue.

Brianna retrieved the vacuum-sealed package from the back of the freezer. The special freezer, the one with the lock, the one she'd told the appliance delivery men was for "expensive cuts." They hadn't asked questions. People rarely did, as long as you offered a reasonable explanation and didn't act suspicious.

The blood salmon thawed quickly under warm water. She'd discovered the technique decades ago. A way to feed without hunting, without harming, without becoming the monster that so many of her kind embraced. The fish were caught, drained, processed, and shipped frozen to a P.O. box she maintained under one of her backup identities. It wasn't cheap, and it wasn't elegant, but it kept her conscience clean.

She hadn't fed from a human in centuries. Hadn't taken a life since the desperate early months after her turning, when she hadn't known any better, when Garth had still been there to teach her control.

Garth.

She pushed the thought away. Some wounds didn't heal, not even after eight centuries.

"Fish?" Mimi inquired, her patience finally fraying.

"Yes, yes." Brianna arranged the salmon on Mimi's plate, the deep red flesh glistening in the morning light. "And it's Wednesday, which means..."

She retrieved the small knife from its case, simple, sharp, well-maintained, and held her forefinger over the plate. A quick incision, barely felt, and several drops of thick, dark blood fell onto the fish.

The wound closed almost before she'd finished, the flesh knitting itself together with the efficiency of eight centuries of cellular memory.

Mimi's eyes fixed on the blood with an intensity that might have been disturbing in any other context. But this was their ritual. Their bond. A few drops of Valensi blood each week, enough to slow the cat's aging to a crawl, to sharpen her senses beyond anything natural, to grant her decades of life that no ordinary feline could claim.

It was, Brianna supposed, the closest thing to a long-term relationship she'd allowed herself since Garth.

"Thanks," Mimi thought, already eating.

"You're welcome, dear friend." Brianna poured herself another cup of coffee. Strong, black, the one human vice she'd never been able to abandon. And leaned against the counter. "Here's to another sixty years."

Mimi didn't respond. She was too busy with the salmon.

Brianna watched her eat and tried not to think about how quiet the kitchen was. How empty the house felt, despite Mimi's presence. How the breakfast table had only one place setting, had only ever had one place setting in this house, in the house before it, in the apartment before that, in the countless homes stretching back through centuries.

She'd made a choice, long ago.

She could still feel the Alpine wind on her face if she let herself remember. The way the snow had stung her cheeks as she'd climbed past the tree line, past the point where even goats refused to go. She'd stood on a granite outcrop with nothing but empty air below and screamed Garth's name until her voice gave out. The mountains had swallowed the sound without echo. Without answer.

Never again, she'd whispered to the wind. *I will never let anyone close enough to lose again.*

The rocks had witnessed. The snow had witnessed. And she had kept that promise for eight hundred years.

It had seemed wise then. Some days it still did.

Other days. Days like this one, with the sun rising and the coffee going cold and no one to share the silence with except a cat who thought in sentence fragments. She wondered if wisdom and loneliness were simply different words for the same thing.

"You're brooding," Mimi observed, licking the last traces of salmon from her whiskers.

"I'm contemplating."

"Same thing. Different word."

Brianna smiled despite herself. "Perhaps you're right."

"Usually am." Mimi hopped down from her bench and padded toward the living room, her tail high with satisfaction. "Going to nap. Don't be sad."

"I'm not sad."

"Liar."

The cat disappeared around the corner, leaving Brianna alone with her coffee and the quiet and the morning light streaming through the windows.

She stood there for a long moment, letting the silence settle around her like a familiar weight. Then she set down her cup, squared her shoulders, and headed for the bedroom to finish getting ready for work.

The mirror showed her a woman of perhaps forty, well-preserved, with dark hair and darker eyes and the kind of bone structure that aged gracefully. The face of Brianna Van Demir, Assistant District Attorney for Mecklenburg County, respected colleague, feared opponent, tireless advocate for justice.

The mask she wore in the daylight world.

She applied her makeup with practiced efficiency. Not because she needed it, but because humans expected it. Foundation to even out skin that was already flawless. Lipstick in a professional shade of mauve. Mascara to define eyes that could see perfectly well in total darkness. The rituals of mortality, performed by a creature who had left mortality behind before the Magna Carta was signed.

Sometimes she wondered what her colleagues would think if they knew. If they could see past the careful performance to the truth beneath. Eight hundred and seventy years of existence, compressed into the shape of a middle-aged lawyer with a good track record and a reputation for preparation.

They'd probably run screaming. Most humans did, when confronted with proof that the monsters were real.

She finished her makeup, selected a charcoal suit from her closet, and dressed with the same efficiency she brought to everything. Armor for the day ahead. Protection against the thousand small interactions that required her to pretend to be something she wasn't.

By the time she emerged from the bedroom, Mimi was curled on the back of the sofa, already half-asleep in a patch of sunlight.

"I'll be back this evening," Brianna said.

"Mmm." Mimi didn't open her eyes. "Bring shrimp."

"I'll see what I can do."

She gathered her briefcase, her keys, her phone. Checked that her sunglasses were in her purse. Habit more than necessity, but some habits died harder than others. Paused at the door to look back at the house she'd built here. The life she'd constructed. The methodical, ordered existence that kept her safe and hidden and utterly, completely alone.

Time to become the District Attorney again, she thought.

Time to pretend.

The sun was fully up now, blazing down from a cloudless October sky. Brianna Van Demir stepped out into the light and didn't burn.

It was going to be a beautiful day.

She wished she could feel something about that.

2

THE DISTRICT ATTORNEY

The beep-woop of the car alarm echoed across the first floor of the parking garage as Brianna made her way toward South McDowell Street.

She enjoyed her morning walk down East Fourth to the rear entrance of the District Attorney's office building. The rhythm of her heels on pavement, the flow of other commuters around her, the particular smell of Charlotte in autumn. Coffee and exhaust and the faint sweetness of dying leaves. She used the time to shift gears, to slide from the quiet solitude of her mornings into the persona she wore at work.

The District Attorney. The advocate. The woman who fought for victims because someone had to.

Climbing the steps between the huge Doric columns, she entered the air-conditioned halls of the Mecklenburg County courthouse complex. The security guards nodded as she passed. They'd learned years ago that Ms. Van Demir arrived early and stayed late and didn't appreciate small talk before her second cup of coffee.

She arrived at her office on the third floor to find the usual Monday chaos already in progress. Phones ringing. Voices overlapping. The particular tension that came from too many cases and not enough hours.

And, as always, a fresh stack of files had materialized on her desk overnight.

"They just keep coming, don't they?" Julie said, peering up from her own desk. The paralegal had been with the Crimes Against Persons team for eight years now. Longer than most lasted before burning out. She had a gift for organization that bordered on the supernatural and a dry wit that Brianna had come to appreciate.

"Like an unwanted rain," Brianna replied, hanging her bag on the coat rack. She began flipping through the new arrivals. Assault. Domestic battery. Sexual assault. Armed robbery with injury. The darker corners of human nature, delivered fresh each morning like a newspaper no one wanted to read.

"How's Mimi?"

"As sassy as ever."

Julie smiled and returned to her docket. She asked about Mimi every morning, had done so ever since Brianna had mentioned the cat in passing years ago. It was the kind of small, consistent kindness that made Julie invaluable. And that made Brianna quietly sad, knowing that eventually she would have to leave this job, this city, these people who had become almost like friends.

Almost. The word did a lot of heavy lifting.

Mark Blomfeld arrived at quarter past eight, coffee in hand, tie slightly askew. He was young, ambitious, and talented enough to justify at least some of his considerable self-confidence. He was also one of the few people in the office who consistently challenged Brianna's conclusions, which she respected even when it irritated her.

"Morning, boss," he said, dropping into his chair.

"I told you not to call me that."

"And yet." He grinned, unrepentant. "Harmon case is closed. Burke took the deal. Eighteen months, anger management, probation."

Brianna kept her expression neutral, but cold disgust settled in her chest. Hank Yeardley had beaten his neighbor nearly to death over a noise complaint. Eighteen months wouldn't teach him anything except how to be more careful next time.

"It's the best we could get," Mark said, reading her silence accurately. "Burke had the self-defense angle locked down. Jury would've been sympathetic."

"I know." She did know. That was the worst part. Eight centuries of watching justice fail to arrive, and she still hadn't made peace with it. "You did good work. We'll get the next one."

Mark nodded, mollified, and turned to his computer. The office settled into its familiar rhythm. Keyboards clicking, phones buzzing, the low murmur of a dozen separate conversations about violence and consequence.

Brianna sorted through her files and tried not to think about all the Hank Yeardleys she'd seen walk free over the centuries.

* * * *

The pre-trial conference was scheduled for ten o'clock.

Brianna arrived at the small conference room five minutes early, case file in hand, her game face firmly in place. Defense counsel was already there. Patricia Holbrook, a public defender with fifteen years of experience and a reputation for tenacity. Her client sat beside her, hands folded on the table, expression carefully blank.

Darren Watts. Twenty-six years old. Charged with aggravated assault after putting his girlfriend in the hospital with a ruptured spleen and three broken ribs. His defense was claiming mutual combat. That she'd attacked him first, that he'd only been defending himself.

The girlfriend, currently recovering in a long-term care facility, told a different story. But she was scared and inconsistent on the stand, and Holbrook knew exactly how to exploit that.

"Ms. Van Demir," Holbrook said, nodding in professional greeting. "I trust you've reviewed our motion?"

"I have." Brianna set her file on the table and took her seat. "And I'm prepared to discuss reasonable alternatives to trial, if your client is willing to accept responsibility for his actions."

Watts's expression didn't change, but contempt flickered in his eyes. Brianna caught it. That brief flash, quickly buried. He thought he was smarter than everyone in this room. Thought he could manipulate his way out of consequences the same way he'd manipulated the woman who loved him.

She'd seen that look before. Hundreds of times. Thousands. The specifics changed, the faces, the names, the centuries, but the look was always the same. Predators wore it like a uniform.

"My client maintains his innocence," Holbrook said. "He was acting in self-defense against an unprovoked attack."

"Your client outweighs the victim by eighty pounds and has a history of violent outbursts documented by three separate employers." Brianna kept her voice level, almost bored. "The medical evidence is inconsistent with mutual combat. The victim's injuries suggest sustained assault, not defensive response."

"The victim has a history of—"

"The victim has a history of being victimized by your client." Brianna met Watts's eyes directly. He didn't look away, but she saw his jaw tighten. "I'm offering five years, with possibility of parole after three. That's generous, given the circumstances."

"That's not—"

"It's also my final offer." She stood, gathering her file. "Take it or leave it, Ms. Holbrook. But if this goes to trial, I'll be asking for the maximum. And I don't lose often."

She left the room without waiting for a response.

In the hallway, she paused to let her pulse settle. She hadn't used any of her abilities in there. No telepathy, no mental pressure, nothing that would have been unfair. She hadn't needed to. Centuries of reading human faces had taught her everything she needed to know about Darren Watts.

He was guilty. He knew it, and now he knew that she knew it.

Whether that would be enough to secure justice remained to be seen.

The new case file was waiting on her desk when she returned from lunch.

It was thinner than most. A fresh arrest, probably from over the weekend. She flipped it open without much expectation. Assault and battery. Male suspect, no priors. Victim was a juvenile, seventeen years old.

She started to set it aside. Mark could handle a simple assault case. And then a phrase caught her eye.

Responding officers noted that the victim appeared disoriented and was "talking about monsters."

Brianna stopped.

She read the line again. Then again.

The report was sparse on details. The responding officers had been more focused on the suspect than the victim's ramblings. But the basics were there: a teenage delivery driver named Marcus Williams, found in an alley off Matheson Avenue in the early hours of Sunday morning, badly beaten, with a head injury consistent with blunt force trauma. The suspect. One John Sebastian Ross, age thirty-two, military veteran, no prior criminal record. Had been found at the scene, covered in blood, with a knife in his hand.

Simple assault. Open and shut.

Except.

Talking about monsters.

Brianna flipped through the rest of the file. Arrest report. Suspect's background check. Military service record. Impressive, actually. Honorable discharge, medical. Currently employed in private security.

No motive listed. No apparent connection between suspect and victim. No witnesses except the victim himself, who had been largely incoherent at the scene and was now under medical observation at Atrium Health.

She turned back to the responding officer's notes. Most of them were routine. Descriptions of the scene, the suspect's demeanor, the victim's injuries. But there, buried in the middle of a paragraph, was another line that made her pulse quicken.

Unidentified residue found at scene. Gray powder, possibly ash. Sent to lab for analysis.

Ash.

In an alley. In the middle of the night. Next to a boy who was talking about monsters.

Brianna closed the file and sat very still.

It could be nothing. Probably was nothing. A traumatized teenager's delusions. Industrial residue from one of the nearby warehouses. A coincidence of language and circumstance that meant exactly what it appeared to mean: a violent assault, a disturbed victim, a suspect with blood on his hands.

But she had lived too long and seen too much to believe in coincidences.

Monsters.

The word echoed in her mind, stirring memories she preferred to keep buried. London. Paris. Berlin. All the places where she'd encountered others of her kind. The ones who didn't bother hiding what they were. The ones who enjoyed the hunt, who saw humans as prey, who left bodies in alleys and didn't care who found them.

The ones Hawthorn called Baneful.

She hadn't thought about that world in years. Had deliberately built a life that kept her far from Valensi politics, Hierarchy machinations, all the dangerous currents that flowed beneath the surface of supernatural society. She had her quiet house and her telepathic cat and her meticulously constructed identity, and she had no desire to risk any of it.

But if there was a Baneful operating in Charlotte. If there was a Hunter tracking them.

She stopped herself. She was jumping to conclusions. Reading significance into coincidence. The boy had been attacked by a human, plain and simple. The "monsters" were trauma-induced hallucinations. The ash was industrial residue.

And the suspect was found with a knife, covered in blood, and no apparent motive.

Brianna drummed her fingers on the file.

She should assign it to Mark. Let him handle the pre-trial motions, the plea negotiations, the tedious mechanics of prosecuting what was probably a straightforward assault case. She had better things to do with her time.

Instead, she pulled the file closer and started reading from the beginning.

John Sebastian Ross. Age thirty-two. Honorable discharge, U.S. Army. Currently employed by...

Her eyes stopped on the employer's name.

Madronite Industries.

She didn't recognize it. Some private security firm, probably. Nothing special.

And yet.

She made a note to look into it later. Then she closed the file, set it aside, and forced herself to focus on the rest of her caseload.

But the word kept echoing in the back of her mind, refusing to be silenced.

Monsters.

She'd look at the file again tonight. After Mimi's dinner. After the sun went down and the house fell silent and she had time to think.

It was probably nothing.

It was almost certainly nothing.

But Brianna Van Demir had learned, over the centuries, to trust her instincts.

And her instincts were telling her that John Sebastian Ross was more than he appeared to be.

3

THE WAITING

The Mecklenburg County Jail had sixty-four cracks in the ceiling of cell block C-7.

Ross knew because he'd counted them. Twice. The first time to have something to do. The second time to verify his count. The Army had taught him that idle hands led to idle minds and idle minds got people killed, so in the absence of a mission he did what he'd always done: gathered intelligence. Mapped his environment. Cataloged assets and liabilities.

Assets: a thin mattress, a scratchy wool blanket, his own body, and the knowledge that Hawthorn monitored police frequencies.

Liabilities: everything else.

Forty-three hours since intake. He'd been processed with brisk efficiency—fingerprints, photograph, property bag. They'd taken the Glock, his wallet, his phone. They hadn't found the second blade strapped beneath the sole of his left boot. Not worth much as a fighting weapon in these quarters, but the weight of it was reassuring. Old habit.

The knife was another matter. His good knife. The Madronite blade he'd slid under the dumpster when he heard the sirens.

He thought about the knife the way he thought about most problems he couldn't currently solve: acknowledged it, filed it, moved on. Someone from Hawthorn would retrieve it. Probably already had. Temper ran a tight operation.

The fact that no one had contacted him yet didn't worry him. Much.

The public defender came on day two.

Twenty-five years old, maybe. Fresh from law school, with bright eyes that were rapidly losing their brightness under the weight of a caseload that would have broken anyone. She'd given him fifteen minutes, handed him a card, and told him they'd talk more when she had time.

She hadn't come back.

Ross didn't blame her. Forty-three hours in a cell had given him time to reconstruct the case from the prosecution's perspective. Suspect found at scene, covered in blood, weapon in hand. Victim alive but badly injured. No witnesses except the victim, who had been incoherent at the scene and would be unreliable at best under cross-examination. The victim's likely account—monsters, a woman with shifting features, a man who appeared from nowhere—would work in Ross's favor as much as it worked against him.

They had enough to charge him. Probably not enough to convict.

The calculation held. He held it steady in his mind like a compass bearing and didn't let himself drift.

On day three, a different man walked through the door.

He wasn't wearing a suit. That was the first tell. The lawyers who'd passed through this block all wore suits, or at least a blazer and tie— the visual shorthand of professional legitimacy. This man wore dark slacks and a quiet gray shirt, and he moved through the cell block with the unhurried confidence of someone who had already determined that nothing in this building could surprise him.

Temper Sloane looked exactly the same as he had ten years ago.

Which was, Ross supposed, one of the stranger aspects of working for an organization whose leadership wasn't entirely human.

"Counselor," Ross said.

"Client." Sloane took the chair across the bolted-down table. His posture was loose, almost bored. His eyes were not. "You're looking well."

"Three days of jail food. Living the dream." Ross kept his voice flat. "The knife?"

"Secure."

"The boy?"

"Stable. Out of ICU as of this morning."

Something in Ross's chest released, just slightly. He didn't let it show. "Good."

"There is," Sloane said, "a complication."

He paused—not for effect; Temper didn't go in for theater—but with the particular hesitation of a man choosing words carefully.

"The unidentified residue. The ash from the scene. The crime lab has it." He set a folded newspaper on the table between them. Code, probably. The kind of tradecraft that felt anachronistic but worked. "Our priority is making sure it goes nowhere. An analysis that raises the right kind of questions in the wrong kind of hands would be—problematic. For all of us."

Ross waited.

"Extraction is in motion. Forty-eight hours. Maybe less." Sloane's tone remained steady, informational. "In the meantime, the priority is keeping the case small. A human-interest story, not a scientific curiosity. To that end." His eyes held Ross's. "If the prosecution approaches you about the Williams boy's account—what he saw, what he heard—the guidance is non-corroboration. Don't confirm the details."

Don't corroborate what Marcus saw.

Ross kept his expression neutral. He was very good at this.

"Understood," he said.

"Good." Sloane stood. "The paperwork is moving. Sit tight."

"That's the plan."

After the guard led Sloane out, Ross sat with his hands folded on the table. The newspaper sat unopened between his elbows.

He thought about Marcus.

Seventeen years old, maybe eighteen. Delivering food for one of those apps, trying to make a few extra dollars. Wrong place, wrong night, wrong alley. He'd been bleeding from the head when Ross knelt beside him, and his eyes had been unfocused and distant, and the things he'd seen that night were going to wake him up screaming for years.

Don't confirm the details.

It was a reasonable operational objective. Protecting Hawthorn's exposure. Keeping the unidentified residue from becoming a news story. Ross understood the logic; he'd been operating inside it for a decade.

He understood the logic the same way he understood a lot of things he didn't particularly like.

The kid had bled on the concrete and believed the monsters were real because they were real. He'd been right. And somewhere inside the machinery of Hawthorn's calculus, that fact was a liability variable, not a person.

Ross picked up the newspaper.

He didn't open it.

He sat there in the institutional light of cell block C-7, counting ceiling cracks in his head until his mind went quiet, and held the weight of the thing he couldn't change and the thing he hadn't walked away from, and he didn't let himself feel it.

He was very good at that, too.

4

THE CALL

The house was quiet when Brianna arrived home.

Mimi was curled on the back of the sofa, exactly where she'd been that morning, though she'd clearly moved at some point. The water bowl in the kitchen was half-empty, and there were fresh claw marks on the scratching post by the window. She opened one amber eye as Brianna set down her briefcase.

"Long day?"

"They're all long days." Brianna crossed to the kitchen and poured herself a glass of wine. A rich Bordeaux she'd been saving for no particular reason. Today felt like reason enough. "Dinner?"

"Already ate. Mouse in the garden." Mimi stretched luxuriously, her claws extending and retracting. "You're tense."

"I'm fine."

"Liar."

Brianna smiled despite herself and carried her wine to the living room. The evening light was fading, painting the walls in shades of amber and rose. She should eat something. Should review the files she'd brought home. Should do any of the hundred small tasks that kept her life running smoothly.

Instead, she sank into the armchair by the window and let herself be still.

The Ross file sat in her briefcase, unopened. She'd meant to look at it again during lunch, but the afternoon had gotten away from her— motions to file, witnesses to prep, the endless machinery of the justice system grinding forward. Now it waited, patient as a predator, and she found herself reluctant to open it.

Monsters.

She took a long sip of wine and watched the last light fade from the sky.

It was probably nothing. A disturbed boy's trauma response. A coincidence of language. She was seeing patterns where none existed, projecting her own history onto circumstances that had nothing to do with her.

And yet.

Madronite Industries.

She still hadn't looked into it. Hadn't wanted to, if she was being honest. Because looking into it meant acknowledging that her instincts might be right. That the careful, quiet life she'd built here might be about to crack open.

That the world she'd spent decades avoiding might have found her anyway.

Mimi hopped down from the sofa and padded over to Brianna's chair, leaping onto the armrest with liquid grace. She settled there, a warm weight against Brianna's arm, and began to purr.

"Whatever it is," the cat thought, "it can wait until tomorrow."

"You're probably right."

"Usually am."

Brianna scratched behind Mimi's ears and let the tension slowly unwind from her shoulders. Tomorrow. She'd deal with it tomorrow. Tonight was for wine and silence and the particular peace that came from being alone in a place that felt like home.

Her phone rang.

She glanced at the screen. Unknown number. Probably a spam call—she'd been getting more of them lately, despite being on every do-not-call list known to man.

She almost didn't answer.

Later, she would think about that moment. The fraction of a second when her finger hovered over the decline button. The future that might have unfolded if she'd simply let it go to voicemail.

But she didn't. Some instinct. The same instinct that had prickled at the Ross file, that had kept her alive for nearly a millennium. Made her accept the call.

"Hello?"

"Brianna."

One word. Her name, spoken in a voice she hadn't heard in over two centuries but would recognize in the depths of hell.

Everything in her went still.

"It's been too long," the voice continued. Cultured. Cold. Carrying an undertone of amusement that made her skin crawl.

Her hand was shaking. She watched it tremble against the arm of the chair as if it belonged to someone else. Mimi had gone rigid beside her, ears flat, responding to something she could sense but Brianna couldn't name.

"Elijah." The name came out as a whisper. She hated how weak it sounded. Hated that after all these years, after everything she'd survived, his voice could still reduce her to this.

"Ah, so you do remember. I'm flattered."

The memories crashed over her like ice water. London. 1799. A gallery opening and a charming stranger and the private rooms of a townhouse where no one could hear her scream. The things he'd done to her. The things he'd said, whispering them into her ear while she couldn't move, couldn't fight, couldn't do anything but endure.

We'll see each other again, Brianna. I've been watching you for a very long time.

She forced herself to breathe. Forced her voice to steady.

"What do you want?"

"So direct. I always appreciated that about you." She could hear the smile in his voice. It made her want to throw the phone across the room. "I'm calling about a situation. A small matter that requires local expertise."

"I don't—"

"There's a Hunter operating in Charlotte." He cut her off as casually as swatting a fly. "He's been quite busy lately. Five confirmed kills in the past three months. The Hierarchy has taken notice."

Brianna's mind raced. A Hunter. In Charlotte. Killing Valensi.

John Sebastian Ross. Madronite Industries. Talking about monsters.

"I've been dispatched to remedy the problem," Elijah continued. "But I could use local assistance. Someone who knows the city. Someone who might help identify the threat before it causes further... embarrassment."

"Why me?"

The question was out before she could stop it. Stupid. She knew why. She'd known the moment she heard his voice.

"Because you're here, darling. Because you've built such a lovely little life in this charming Southern city. Because you have access to information that could prove useful." A pause. "And because I know you'll want to help. Given the alternative."

There it was. The threat, wrapped in silk and delivered with a smile.

"I don't know anything about a Hunter."

"Then perhaps you should look into it. I believe the local authorities recently arrested someone who might be of interest. A man named Ross, I think? Involved in some unfortunate business with a delivery boy."

Her blood ran cold.

He knew. He already knew about the case file. About Ross. About all of it.

"How did you—"

"I have resources, Brianna. Surely you remember that." His voice dropped, losing some of its false warmth. "I'll be in touch again tomorrow. I expect you'll have something useful to share by then. Don't disappoint me."

The line went dead.

Brianna sat motionless in her chair, the phone still pressed to her ear, listening to silence.

Mimi nudged her arm. "Bri? Bri, you're scaring me."

She couldn't respond. Couldn't move. Couldn't do anything but sit there while her painstakingly constructed world crumbled around her.

Elijah was here. In Charlotte. Looking for Ross.

And he expected her to help him.

* * * *

She didn't know how long she sat there before her body started working again.

Minutes, probably. Maybe longer. The wine glass had slipped from her fingers at some point, spilling red across the hardwood floor like blood. She stared at it without really seeing it.

We'll see each other again.

He'd promised her that, two hundred and twenty-six years ago. Promised it while she lay broken and bleeding on the floor of his townhouse, while he straightened his cravat and smiled down at her with those empty, ancient eyes. She'd fled London that night. Fled England entirely. Spent the next century burning herself in the sun, over and over, building the tolerance that would let her walk in daylight while the rest of her kind slept.

All to hide from him.

And now he was here.

"Bri." Mimi's voice was insistent, worried. The cat had jumped down from the armrest and was pacing in front of her, tail lashing. "What happened? Who was that?"

"Someone I used to know."

"Bad someone?"

Brianna laughed. A harsh, broken sound that had nothing to do with humor. "The worst someone."

She made herself stand. Made herself walk to the kitchen, find paper towels, clean up the spilled wine. The mechanical actions helped. Gave her something to focus on besides the fear that was trying to swallow her whole.

Think, she told herself. You've survived worse than this. You've survived him before.

But she hadn't, really. She'd run. She'd hidden. She'd built a life on the other side of an ocean and pretended that if she stayed quiet enough, invisible enough, he would forget about her.

He hadn't forgotten.

I've been watching you for a very long time.

She threw the wine-soaked paper towels in the trash and gripped the edge of the counter, forcing herself to breathe.

Elijah wanted her to help him find Ross. To identify the Hunter, track his patterns, hand him over to a Protector who would tear him apart without a second thought.

And if she refused?

Because you've built such a lovely little life in this charming Southern city.

She thought of Julie, asking about Mimi every morning. Of Mark, calling her "boss" even when she told him not to. Of the security guards who nodded when she passed, the baristas who knew her coffee order, the dozens of small connections that made up a life.

She thought of Daphne.

Daphne.

If Elijah knew about her job, about the Ross case, then he knew about the rest of it too. Knew about the house. The routines. The people she saw, the places she went, everything that made her vulnerable.

He knew about Daphne.

Brianna closed her eyes and felt resolve crystallize in her chest, cold and hard.

She couldn't run. Not this time. Running meant leaving everything behind. The job, the house, the measured life she'd built here. It meant abandoning the people who depended on her, however distantly. It meant letting Elijah win.

There was *one* person who might know what Elijah's presence in Charlotte meant — a Solari named Brenda Shields, based in D.C., with connections to the Hierarchy that Brianna had spent years deliberately not asking about. She'd avoided that particular debt for decades. It looked like that was over. Perhaps. Might not be wise to involve Brenda yet.

But she couldn't help Elijah either. Ross, whoever he was, whatever he was, had saved a boy's life. Had killed a Baneful who was hunting teenagers in alleys. He wasn't a murderer. He was a defender.

And Elijah wanted her to help destroy him.

She opened her eyes and stared at her reflection in the darkened window. The woman staring back looked older than she felt. Older than she had any right to look.

What are you going to do?

She didn't have an answer.

Not yet.

But as she stood there in her quiet kitchen, with Mimi watching anxiously from the doorway and the night pressing in against the windows, one thing became absolutely clear:

The ordered life of Brianna Van Demir, Assistant District Attorney, was over.

Whatever came next would require her to be something else entirely.

5

THE GALLERY

LONDON, 1799

Six hundred and forty-seven years.

That was how long Brianna had been Valensi when she met Elijah for the first time. Six centuries of survival. Of hiding. Of building lives and abandoning them, wearing names like costumes and shedding them when they no longer fit.

She had become skilled at disappearing.

London in 1799 was a city of contradictions. Elegant townhouses rising beside open sewers, grand theaters playing to audiences who stepped over beggars on their way inside. The industrial revolution was reshaping the world, and Brianna had positioned herself to watch it happen from a comfortable distance.

She worked as a nurse at Guy's Hospital, tending to the sick and dying with a patience that her colleagues attributed to saintliness but was really just the product of having seen too much death to be moved by it anymore. She had a small room in a boarding house near Southwark, kept to herself, attended church on Sundays because it was expected. A quiet life. An invisible life.

Exactly what she wanted.

She had learned, over the centuries, to recognize others of her kind. There was a particular quality to the way Valensi moved, a stillness beneath the surface that no amount of practice could entirely conceal. London had its share of them. The city was old enough and dark enough to attract those who preferred shadows. But Brianna avoided them carefully. She had no interest in Valensi politics, in Hierarchy machinations, in the endless games of power and territory that consumed so many of her kind.

She wanted only to be left alone.

The gallery opening was a mistake.

She shouldn't have gone. The invitation had come through one of the doctors at the hospital. A social nicety, nothing more, easily declined. But she'd been in London for twelve years, and the walls of her small room had begun to feel like a prison, and some reckless part of her had whispered that one evening among humans couldn't possibly hurt.

That reckless part had been wrong.

The Harrington Gallery occupied a Georgian townhouse in Mayfair, its rooms transformed for the evening into a showcase of fashionable art and fashionable people. Brianna arrived in a borrowed dress. Dark green silk, modest but well-made. And accepted a glass of wine she had no intention of drinking.

She moved through the crowd like a ghost, observing without engaging. The paintings were mediocre, the conversation worse. She was already planning her escape when she felt someone watching her.

Not the casual glances she was accustomed to. Men assessing her figure, women evaluating her dress. But something more focused. More intent. The particular attention of a predator recognizing another predator.

She turned.

He was standing by the fireplace, a glass of brandy in one hand, his posture relaxed in a way that spoke of absolute confidence. Perhaps thirty in appearance, with dark hair and darker eyes and features that belonged on a Roman coin. Handsome, certainly. But that wasn't what made her breath catch.

It was the age in his eyes. The weight of centuries, poorly hidden behind a mask of urbane charm.

He was Valensi. Old Valensi. Far older than her.

She should have left then. Should have set down her wine and walked out the door and never looked back. Every instinct she'd honed over six centuries was screaming at her to run.

But he was already crossing the room toward her, and something, pride perhaps, or simple stubbornness, kept her feet rooted to the floor.

"Forgive my forwardness," he said, his voice cultured and warm. "But I couldn't help noticing you across the room. You have the look of someone who would rather be anywhere else."

"Is it that obvious?"

"Only to someone paying attention." He smiled, and despite everything, she felt herself respond to it. He had the kind of smile that made you want to trust him. "I'm Elijah."

"Brianna."

"A pleasure, Brianna." He said her name like he was tasting it. "Tell me—what brings a woman of such obvious refinement to a gallery showing work of such obvious mediocrity?"

She laughed before she could stop herself. "A moment of weakness. And you?"

"The same, I suppose." His eyes never left hers. "Though I find myself suddenly grateful for the impulse."

They talked for hours.

He was charming in a way that felt effortless. Asking questions about her life, her work, her opinions on art and literature and the state of the world. He listened with what seemed like genuine interest, offering his own observations with wit and intelligence. He made her feel seen in a way she hadn't felt since.

Since Garth.

She pushed that thought away. Garth had been gone for over eight centuries now, vanished without explanation on an autumn morning in 1225. She had searched for decades. Had never stopped hoping, not entirely, that someday she might learn what had happened to him.

But hope was a luxury she couldn't afford. Not here. Not with this stranger whose eyes held secrets she couldn't read.

Still, Elijah wasn't asking to be close. He was simply... pleasant. Engaging. A few hours of conversation with someone who understood what it meant to live outside of time.

What harm could it do?

The gallery closed at midnight. The other guests filtered out into the foggy London streets, their laughter fading into the darkness. Brianna was reaching for her cloak when Elijah appeared beside her.

"I have a carriage waiting," he said. "May I offer you a ride home?"

She should have said no.

"That's very kind of you."

The carriage was elegant: black lacquer and brass fittings, drawn by matched grays that stamped impatiently in the cold. He handed her up with perfect courtesy, then settled onto the seat across from her.

"Where to?"

She gave him the address of her boarding house. He relayed it to the driver, and the carriage lurched into motion.

For a few minutes, they rode in comfortable silence. The city slid past the windows: gas lamps flickering in the fog, shadows pooling in doorways. Brianna watched it pass and wondered why her heart was beating faster.

"You're nervous," Elijah observed.

"Should I be?"

"That depends." He leaned forward, his eyes catching the light from a passing lamp. His expression had shifted. The warmth remained, but beneath it she could see what had been hidden all evening. Something cold and hungry and very, very old. "On what you're willing to do to survive the next hour."

The carriage turned.

Wrong direction. They should have been heading south, toward Southwark. Instead, they were going north. Toward Mayfair. Toward the wealthy townhouses where men like Elijah made their homes.

"Let me out." Her voice came out steadier than she felt. "Now."

"I don't think so." He was still smiling, but the charm had fallen away like a discarded mask. What remained was something she recognized from her darkest moments: the face of a predator who had cornered his prey. "We have so much to discuss, you and I."

She reached for the door. His hand closed around her wrist, fast, impossibly fast, and she felt the bones grind together under his grip.

"Don't," he said softly. "You'll only make it worse."

The townhouse was beautiful.

She registered that fact distantly, the way you might notice the weather while walking to your own execution. High ceilings. Crystal chandeliers. Paintings that were worth more than most people earned in a lifetime.

Elijah led her through the foyer and up a sweeping staircase, his grip on her arm never loosening. She could have fought. Could have screamed, struggled, tried to break free. But she'd felt his strength when he'd grabbed her wrist. He was older than her by centuries, maybe millennia. Fighting would only delay the inevitable.

And she had learned, over six hundred years, to recognize when she was outmatched.

The room he took her to was a study of some kind. Leather chairs, a massive desk, bookshelves lining the walls. He released her arm and crossed to a sideboard, pouring himself a drink with the casual ease of a man in complete control.

"Sit," he said, gesturing to one of the chairs.

She didn't move.

He turned to look at her, and amusement flickered in his eyes. Or perhaps annoyance. It was hard to tell with him. Hard to read anything beneath the mask.

"I said sit."

Her legs folded beneath her. Not because she chose to obey. Because he made her. His will pressing against hers like a physical weight, forcing her body to comply even as her mind screamed in protest.

Telepathy. Stronger than anything she'd ever encountered. Strong enough to override her own control of her limbs.

"There," he said, satisfaction curling through his voice. "That's better."

He circled behind her chair, and she felt his fingers trail across her shoulders. Light. Almost gentle. The touch of a man who knew exactly how much fear he was causing and savored every moment of it.

"I've been watching you for a very long time, Brianna." His breath was warm against her ear. "Did you know that? Decades. Centuries, even. You've been so very careful. So very quiet. Building your little lives, abandoning them, always staying one step ahead of anyone who might notice you."

She didn't speak. Didn't move. She only sit there, stymied at her next move, while he whispered horrors into her ear.

"You're interesting to me. Do you understand what that means? How rare it is for someone like me to find anything... interesting... after so many years?"

His hand closed around her throat. Not squeezing. Just... holding. A reminder of how easily he could end her.

"You've been alone for a long time, haven't you? Ever since that husband of yours vanished." He felt her flinch and laughed softly. "Oh yes, I know about him. I know about a great many things. The Hierarchy keeps very thorough records."

Garth. He knew about Garth. The old wound tore open, spilling grief she'd thought she'd buried centuries ago.

"Still searching, after all this time?" His voice dripped with false sympathy. "Yet hoping he might walk through a door someday? How... touching."

She found her voice, though it came out as barely a whisper. "What do you want?"

"Want?" He released her throat and circled back around to face her, that terrible smile still playing at his lips. "I want to be entertained. I want something to occupy my attention during the long, tedious centuries. And you, my dear Brianna, are going to provide that entertainment."

"I won't—"

"You will." He crouched in front of her chair, his face level with hers, those ancient eyes boring into her own. "You don't understand yet, but you will. I'm not going to kill you, Brianna. Death is too quick. Too simple." He reached out and touched her cheek, almost tenderly. "I'm going to teach you what you really are. What you've been hiding from all these centuries. And when I'm finished..."

He leaned closer. His lips brushed her ear.

"You'll thank me for it."

The first day was the worst.

Or perhaps it only felt that way because she still believed she might escape. Thought, in some naive corner of her mind, that this was something she could survive intact.

He didn't bind her. Didn't need to. His telepathy was a cage more effective than any rope or chain. She could feel it pressing against her mind. A constant weight, a presence that monitored her every thought, her every impulse. When she tried to move toward the door, her legs simply stopped working. When she tried to scream, her voice died in her throat.

"There's no point fighting it," he told her, watching her struggle with clinical interest. "I've been doing this for three thousand years. You're not the first to try. You won't be the last."

Three thousand years. The number hit her like a blow. She'd thought herself old at six centuries. Experienced. Wise. But this creature in front of her had lived five times as long. Had perfected cruelties she couldn't imagine.

And he had all the time in the world.

"Let me explain how this is going to work," he said, settling into a chair across from her with the ease of a man about to discuss the weather. "I'm going to take things from you. Control. Dignity. The pleasant little lies you've told yourself about what you are." He smiled. "And you're going to let me. Not because you want to. Though you might, eventually. But because you have no other choice."

"Why?" The word scraped out of her throat. "Why me?"

"Because you think you're different." He leaned forward, genuine interest flickering in his eyes. "Most Valensi accept what they are within a century or two. They embrace the predator. The hunger. The power. But you..." He shook his head slowly. "Six hundred years, and you're still pretending to be human. Working as a nurse, helping the sick and dying, as if that somehow makes you less of a monster."

"I'm not—"

"You are." His voice cracked like a whip. "We all are. That's what the Birthing does. It strips away the human weakness and leaves something purer behind. Something stronger. But you've been fighting it. Suppressing it. Pretending you can still be the girl who lived in Lyon, the woman who fell in love with Garth Van Demir."

He said Garth's name like he was handling something delicate. Something he intended to break.

"You don't know anything about me."

"I know everything about you." He rose from his chair and crossed to her, his footsteps deliberate on the hardwood floor. "I know you Birthed young. Eighteen, yes? In the flower of youth, as they used to say. I know you loved your husband with a devotion that survived his disappearance. I know you've spent six centuries building lives you never let yourself care about, because caring hurts too much."

He stopped in front of her. Reached down and lifted her chin, forcing her to meet his eyes.

"I know you're lonely, Brianna. Desperately, achingly lonely. And I know that beneath all that careful control, there's a part of you that wants to let go. To stop pretending. To be what you were made to be."

"You're wrong."

"Am I?" His thumb traced along her jawline. "We'll see."

She lost track of time.

Day bled into night bled into day again, and Brianna couldn't tell anymore where one ended and the next began. There were no windows in the room he kept her in. Or rather, there were windows, but heavy curtains blocked any light that might have given her a reference point. She existed in a kind of twilight, measured only by the intervals between his visits.

He came to her in waves. Sometimes he was gentle, almost kind, bringing food she couldn't taste, wine she couldn't swallow, speaking to her in soft tones about art, philosophy, the nature of power. During these moments, she could almost forget what he was doing. Could almost pretend this was just a strange sort of captivity, unpleasant but survivable.

Then the gentleness would stop.

He never raised his voice. That was the worst part. Even when he was hurting her. And he hurt her, in ways that would have killed a human twice over. His voice remained calm. Conversational. As if he were discussing the finer points of wine selection while his fingers found the places that made her scream.

"Pain is honest," he told her once, watching her body knit itself back together. "It shows you what you really are."

She was crying. She didn't remember starting, but the tears were there, tracking down her cheeks, dripping onto the ruined silk of her dress.

"Do you know what I see, Brianna?" He crouched beside her, tilting his head like a curious bird. "Potential. You could be magnificent, if you'd stop clinging to your humanity."

"I don't—" Her voice cracked. "I don't want to be magnificent."

"Yes, you do." He smiled that terrible smile. "You just don't know it yet."

The worst moments weren't the physical ones.

She could survive pain. Had survived it before. The Birthing itself had been agony, her human body dying and being remade over three days of fever and screaming. She had learned, over six centuries, to endure what her flesh was subjected to. To retreat into some quiet corner of her mind and wait for the healing to begin.

But Elijah didn't just hurt her body.

He hurt her mind.

His telepathy let him see everything: every memory, every fear, every secret she'd buried in the depths of her consciousness. And he used them. Weaponized them. Made her relive moments she'd spent centuries trying to forget.

Garth's face on their wedding night. The sound of his laugh. The way he'd held her after her Birthing, stroking her hair while the fever burned through her, promising that everything would be all right.

Elijah pulled those memories out of her like threads from a tapestry, examined them with clinical precision, and then *twisted* them. Made her see Garth's face contorted in disgust. Made her hear his voice saying things he never would have said. That she was a monster, a predator, that he'd been right to leave her.

"Stop," she begged. "Please, stop—"

"Why?" He seemed genuinely curious. "These are your memories. Your feelings. I'm just helping you see them clearly."

"They're not—he never—"

"How do you know?" He leaned close, his voice soft as arsenic. "You never found him. Never learned what happened. How do you know he didn't leave because he finally saw what you really are?"

She couldn't answer. Couldn't think. Could only lie there, her mind shredded, her certainties crumbling, while Elijah whispered doubt into the spaces where her identity used to be.

Somewhere in the second night, or was it the third, she stopped fighting.

Not consciously. It wasn't a decision. It was simply... exhaustion. The cumulative weight of everything he'd done, everything he'd shown her, everything he'd made her feel. She didn't have the strength to resist anymore. Didn't have the will.

He noticed immediately.

"There," he said, and there was something almost gentle in his voice. "That wasn't so hard, was it?"

She didn't respond. Couldn't. She was floating somewhere outside herself, watching from a distance as he arranged her limbs, positioned her body, used her as if she were a doll he'd grown tired of pretending was real.

"You understand now, don't you?" His breath was warm against her ear. "What you are. What you've always been."

She didn't understand anything. She was empty. Hollow. A shell of a person wearing the face of someone who used to be Brianna Van Demir.

"Say it."

She didn't know what he wanted her to say. Didn't care. Her lips moved anyway, forming words she couldn't hear, giving him whatever answer would make this stop.

"Good." He pressed a kiss to her forehead. Tender, almost loving. "You're learning."

She woke to silence.

For a long moment, she didn't move. Didn't breathe. Just lay there on the floor, when had she ended up on the floor, waiting for the next wave of horror to begin.

Nothing happened.

Slowly, painfully, she opened her eyes.

The room was empty. The heavy curtains had been pulled back, and gray morning light was filtering through the windows. The first natural light she'd seen in... how long? Three days? Four? She couldn't remember.

Her body was a ruin. She could feel the wounds. Dozens of them, in various stages of healing. Some had closed over completely, leaving nothing but smooth skin. Others were still raw, weeping blood that was already beginning to clot. Her dress was destroyed, more blood and torn fabric than clothing.

But she was alive.

And she was alone.

She tried to stand. Her legs buckled. She tried again, using the wall for support, and managed to get upright. Every movement sent pain lancing through her, but she ignored it. Pain was familiar now. Pain was almost a friend.

The door was unlocked.

She stared at it for a long moment, not understanding. He'd kept her caged with his mind for days. Why would he leave the physical door open? Unless...

Unless he wanted her to leave.

The realization hit her like cold water. This wasn't escape. This was *release*. He'd taken what he wanted, done what he'd set out to do, and now he was letting her go. Like a cat releasing a mouse it had grown bored of tormenting.

She should have felt relief. Should have felt grateful that it was over.

Instead, she felt nothing at all.

He was waiting for her in the foyer.

Of course he was. He hadn't left. Had simply withdrawn his presence from her mind, let her wake on her own, let her believe for one precious moment that she might walk out of this without a final encounter.

"Leaving so soon?" He was dressed impeccably, as if the past three days had never happened. As if he hadn't spent them systematically destroying everything she thought she knew about herself.

She didn't answer. Couldn't find words that mattered.

"I want you to understand something." He crossed to her, and she flinched, couldn't help it, but he only reached out and straightened the torn collar of her dress. A mockery of tenderness. "This isn't over. It will never be over. I'll always know where you are. I'll always be watching."

"Why?" Her voice came out as a rasp.

"Because you're mine now." He said it simply, as if stating an obvious fact. "You've always been mine. You just didn't know it yet. Now you do."

"I'm not—"

"You are." His fingers caught her chin, forced her to meet his eyes. "Part of you will always be in that room. Part of you will always be the creature I showed you. And someday. Maybe tomorrow, maybe a century from now. I'm going to come for you again. And you're going to let me, because by then you'll understand that fighting is pointless."

He released her. Stepped back. Smiled that terrible, charming smile.

"Run along now, darling. Go back to your little life. Pretend this never happened." His eyes gleamed. Amusement or anticipation, she couldn't tell which. Perhaps both. "I'll be seeing you."

She walked out the door without looking back.

She didn't run. Didn't cry. Just walked. One foot in front of the other, through the streets of Mayfair, past the elegant townhouses where monsters made their homes. The sun was rising, and she should have been seeking shelter, should have been afraid of the light, but she couldn't bring herself to care.

Let it burn her. Let it turn her to ash. At least then she'd be free.

But the sun didn't burn her. Not yet. The clouds were thick enough to diffuse the light, and she made it to the docks while the sky was still gray.

She found a ship bound for Lisbon. Traded her remaining jewelry. A ring that had been her mother's, a necklace Garth had given her on their wedding night. For passage in the cargo hold. The captain didn't ask questions. Didn't seem to notice the blood, the torn dress, the empty look in her eyes.

Or maybe he noticed and simply didn't care.

She spent the crossing huddled in the darkness, healing wounds that should have been fatal, trying to piece together what remained of herself.

The physical damage faded within days. Valensi healed fast, and she'd survived worse injuries in the early years after her Birthing. The cuts closed. The bruises faded. Even the deeper wounds, the ones that had reached bone, eventually sealed themselves shut.

The other damage would take longer.

She could still feel him. That was the worst part. Even with an ocean between them, she could feel his presence at the edges of her mind. Faint, distant, but unmistakably there. A reminder that he had been inside her head. That he knew her now, in ways no one else ever had.

That he could find her whenever he chose.

She lay in the darkness of the cargo hold, listening to the creak of the ship, the slap of waves against the hull, and she thought about what he'd said. *Part of you will always be in that room. Part of you will always be the creature I showed you.*

Was it true? Was she different now? Broken in some fundamental way that would never heal?

She didn't know. Couldn't tell anymore where she ended and the damage began.

But somewhere in that darkness. Somewhere between the pain and the fear and the terrible weight of what had been done to her. A decision began to form.

She couldn't fight him. He was too old, too strong, too deeply embedded in the Hierarchy's power structure. Running was futile. He'd made it clear that he could find her whenever he chose.

But she could hide in a way he wouldn't expect.

Valensi couldn't walk in daylight. It was their greatest weakness, the thing that forced them into the shadows, that made them vulnerable during the long hours between dawn and dusk. Elijah slept during the day, like all of their kind. Which meant he couldn't follow her into the light.

But there were stories. Whispers. Tales of Valensi who had somehow overcome that weakness. Who had burned themselves, over and over, building a tolerance to the sun through sheer, agonizing repetition.

The process took decades. Sometimes centuries. Most who attempted it went mad long before they succeeded.

But if she could do it. If she could walk in daylight while Elijah and his kind slept. Then she could build a life in the sun where he couldn't follow. Could hide in the one place he would never think to look.

It would hurt.

It would nearly destroy her.

But she had nothing left to lose.

The ship docked in Lisbon three weeks later.

Brianna walked down the gangplank into the gray morning light, feeling the wind on her face. The clouds were thinning. Soon, dawn's light would be strong enough to burn.

She thought about Elijah. About his smile. About the things he'd whispered in the darkness.

Part of you will always be the creature I showed you.

Maybe he was right. Maybe some part of her was broken beyond repair. Maybe she would spend the rest of eternity carrying the weight of those three days, feeling his presence at the edge of her mind, waiting for him to come for her again.

But she was still standing. Still breathing. Still here.

And if she was going to be a creature of the darkness, then she would become something else. Something that could survive in the light. Something he couldn't touch.

The clouds parted.

A single ray of sunlight fell across the dock, warm and golden and deadly.

Brianna Van Demir stepped into it and let herself burn.

The pain was indescribable. Fire in her blood, her skin blistering, every cell in her body screaming for her to seek shelter. But she didn't move. Didn't retreat. Just stood there, burning, while the sun carved its way across the morning sky.

When she finally staggered into the shadows. Skin blackened, body smoking, barely conscious. She was laughing.

It would take a hundred years. A hundred years of burning, of agony, of forcing herself to endure what should have been unendurable.

But she would do it. She would become Solari.

And when Elijah came for her again. Because he would, she knew he would. She would be waiting for him.

In the light.

6

THE WITNESS

The address in the case file led Brianna to a garden apartment complex off Central Avenue, the kind of place where working families stretched paychecks to cover rent and hoped nothing broke that they couldn't fix themselves.

She parked her car in the visitor lot and sat for a moment, gathering herself.

She'd barely slept. Every time she closed her eyes, she was back in that London townhouse, feeling Elijah's fingers on her throat, hearing his voice whisper promises she'd spent two centuries trying to forget. The morning had been a blur of coffee and routine, her body going through the motions while her mind raced in circles.

What are you going to do?

She still didn't have an answer. But she had a lead. A boy who'd been talking about monsters. A case file that didn't add up.

If she was going to make a decision about Ross, about Elijah, she needed to know the truth first.

The Williams family lived in unit 14B, ground floor, with a small concrete patio that held two plastic chairs and a dying fern. Brianna straightened her blazer, checked that her DA credentials were visible, and knocked.

The woman who answered was perhaps forty, with tired eyes and the kind of wariness that came from too many unexpected visitors bringing bad news. She looked at Brianna's credentials, then at Brianna's face, then back at the credentials again.

"I already talked to the police," she said.

"I know, Mrs. Williams. I'm with the District Attorney's office. I'm handling the case against the man who hurt your son, and I'd like to ask Marcus a few questions if he's feeling up to it."

The wariness deepened. "The doctors said he needs rest. Said talking about it might make the trauma worse."

"I understand. I'll keep it brief, and I'll stop the moment he seems distressed. But Marcus is our only witness to what happened that night. His testimony could be crucial."

It was the truth, if not the whole truth. What Brianna really needed couldn't be found in any official testimony.

Mrs. Williams hesitated, then stepped aside. "Five minutes. And I'm staying in the room."

"Of course."

Marcus was sitting up in bed when Brianna entered, a laptop open on his knees, headphones around his neck. The bandage on his head was smaller than she'd expected, the wound must be healing well, but the look in his eyes was anything but healed.

He had the hollow stare of someone who'd seen something that didn't fit into the world as he understood it. Brianna recognized that look. She'd worn it herself, once, a very long time ago.

"Marcus, this is Ms. Van Demir from the DA's office," his mother said. "She has some questions about what happened."

"I already told the cops." His voice was flat, defensive. "They didn't believe me."

"I'm not the police." Brianna pulled one of the plastic chairs from the corner and sat down, keeping her posture open and unthreatening. "And I'm not here to judge what you saw. I'm here to listen."

He held her gaze, something flickering behind those hollow eyes. Hope, maybe. Or just the desperate need to be believed.

"Mom, can you give us a minute?"

Mrs. Williams frowned. "I told her I was staying—"

"Please. Just... please."

The conflict played across his mother's face. The need to protect warring with the recognition that her son needed something she couldn't give him. Finally, she nodded.

"I'll be right outside. You call if you need me."

When the door closed, Marcus seemed to deflate slightly, the tension leaving his shoulders. He closed the laptop and set it aside, then looked at Brianna with an intensity that belied his seventeen years.

"You're going to think I'm crazy."

"Try me."

He took a breath. "There was a woman. Following me."

"Following you where?"

"From the restaurant. I do deliveries for this app, you know? Late night stuff, when the tips are better. I'd just dropped off an order and I was walking back to my bike, and I saw her. Just... standing there. Watching me."

"What did she look like?"

"Pretty. Like, really pretty. Dark hair, pale skin. The kind of pretty that makes you nervous, you know? Like something's wrong but you can't figure out what."

Brianna kept her expression neutral, but her pulse quickened. She knew exactly what he meant.

"I tried to ignore her," Marcus continued. "Kept walking. But every time I looked back, she was closer. Not running or anything. Just... closer. Like the distance didn't mean anything to her."

"What happened then?"

"I panicked. Turned down this side street, thought maybe I could lose her. Stupid. It was a dead end." He laughed bitterly. "Dead end. That's exactly what it almost was."

"She cornered you?"

"She was just there. One second the alley was empty, the next she was right in front of me. Smiling. And her face..." He trailed off, his hands twisting in the bedsheet.

"What about her face, Marcus?"

"It changed." The words came out as barely a whisper. "Her eyes got darker, and her mouth... she had these teeth. Not normal teeth. And she said—" He swallowed hard. "She said I smelled delicious."

Brianna felt the cold certainty settle into her chest. Baneful. A Baneful had been hunting this boy, playing with him the way a cat played with a mouse before the kill.

"What happened next?"

"The guy showed up. The one they arrested. He came out of nowhere, yelled at her to step away from me. She laughed at him. Said something I didn't understand. And then they... fought."

"Fought how?"

"Fast. Too fast. I couldn't even follow what was happening. She hit him, he hit her, there was blood everywhere. I tried to run, but she—" His hand went to his head, touching the bandage. "She grabbed me. Threw me. I hit something, and then everything went dark for a while."

"But you saw the end of it?"

Marcus nodded slowly. "I woke up, and she was... screaming. This horrible sound, like nothing I've ever heard. And then she just... fell apart. Like she was made of ash and someone blew on her." He looked at Brianna with desperate, pleading eyes. "That happened. I know how it sounds, but that happened. She was there, and then she wasn't, and the guy, Ross, he was just standing over this pile of dust, bleeding everywhere, and I know I hit my head but I wasn't imagining it, I wasn't—"

"Marcus." Brianna leaned forward and caught his gaze. "I believe you."

He stopped. Stared at her. "You... what?"

"I believe you. What you saw was real."

The tears came without warning. Silent, streaming down his face as some dam inside him finally broke. He'd been carrying this alone, the terror of what he'd witnessed compounded by the certainty that no one would ever believe him.

"What was she?" he asked. "What the fuck was that thing?"

Brianna weighed her answer. The truth was dangerous. The truth could get him killed, if he talked to the wrong people. But he'd already seen enough that lies wouldn't help him heal.

"There are things in this world that most people never see," she said finally. "Predators that wear human faces. They've existed for a very long time, hidden in the shadows, and most of them follow rules that keep them hidden. But some of them don't. Some of them hunt for pleasure."

"Like her."

"Like her. And there are people who hunt them. People who try to protect others from the ones who've stopped following the rules."

"The guy. Ross. He's one of those people?"

Brianna thought about the case file. The military background. The connection to Madronite Industries. The knife that had turned a Valensi to ash.

"I think so. Yes."

Marcus was quiet for a long moment, processing. Then: "So he saved my life."

"It looks that way."

"But they arrested him. They think he hurt me."

"The police don't know what you know. They can't see what you saw." Brianna paused, choosing her next words with care. "Marcus, what happened that night, what you witnessed, you can never talk about it. Not to the police, not to your mother, not to anyone."

"Why not? If Ross is innocent—"

"Because the things that hunt in the dark don't like being exposed. If word gets out that you know about them, that you can identify them, you become a target. And there are things far worse than the woman in that alley."

She saw the fear flicker back into his eyes, but alongside it was something harder. Understanding. He'd looked into the darkness and survived, and now he was being asked to carry that knowledge alone.

"What do I tell people?"

"You tell them you don't remember. Head trauma. The doctors will back you up. Memory loss is common with injuries like yours. You tell them the last thing you recall is walking to your bike, and the next thing you knew, you were in the hospital."

"And Ross?"

"Let me worry about Ross."

Marcus nodded. He seemed smaller somehow, younger, the weight of secrets already pressing down on his shoulders. Brianna recognized that weight. She'd been carrying her own for eight centuries.

She reached out and touched his hand. Just briefly, just enough to establish contact. And as she did, she pushed, gently, at the edges of his mind. Not erasing anything. Not changing what he knew. Just... smoothing. Softening the sharpest edges of the terror. Making it easier to bury, to set aside, to keep hidden in the locked rooms of his memory where it couldn't hurt him.

It was a violation, in its own way. A small theft of autonomy, even if it was meant kindly.

But she'd seen what happened to humans who couldn't forget. She'd watched them break under the weight of knowledge they were never meant to carry. If a little mental adjustment could spare Marcus that fate, she'd make that choice and carry the guilt herself.

She had plenty of practice.

"Thank you for talking to me," she said, rising from the chair. "Take care of yourself, Marcus. Stay in the light."

He looked up at her, and for just a moment, she thought he understood more than he should. More than any seventeen-year-old should have to understand.

"You're not like the other lawyers, are you?"

She allowed herself a small smile. "No. I suppose I'm not."

She sat in her car for a long time after leaving the Williams apartment.

The pieces were falling into place now, forming a picture she didn't want to see. Ross wasn't a murderer. He was a Hunter. One of Hawthorn's people, apparently, given his connection to Madronite. He'd killed a Baneful who was preying on teenagers in Charlotte. He'd saved Marcus's life.

And Elijah wanted him dead.

I expect you'll have something useful to share by then. Don't disappoint me.

She could lie. Tell Elijah she'd investigated and found nothing— just a random assault, no supernatural elements, nothing to concern the Hierarchy. Ross was in custody; he wasn't a threat. Let Elijah chase shadows while the real Hunter sat safely in a jail cell.

But Elijah had resources. Connections. If he was already watching her closely enough to know about the case file, he might have other sources too. He might find out she'd visited Marcus. Might learn what questions she'd asked.

And if he discovered she'd lied to him...

We'll see each other again. I'll always know where you are.

She gripped the steering wheel until her knuckles went white.

She couldn't hand Ross over to Elijah. The man had saved a boy's life. Whatever else he was, whatever methods he used, he was fighting the same monsters Brianna had spent centuries hiding from. He didn't deserve to die for that.

But she couldn't defy Elijah directly either. Not yet. Not without a plan, without allies, without something more than desperate hope.

She needed more information. About Ross. About Hawthorn. About whatever the hell Madronite Industries actually was.

And she needed to figure out what she was willing to risk to do the right thing.

Her phone buzzed. A text from Daphne: Still on for dinner? I'm bringing extra shrimp for Fancy Pants.

Brianna stared at the message.

Daphne. Sweet, patient, stubborn Daphne, who had waited seven years for Brianna to let her in. Who had no idea what kind of danger was circling closer with every passing hour.

Chinese sounds perfect, she typed back. See you at seven.

She put the phone away and started the car.

One thing at a time. One step at a time. That was how you survived centuries.

That was how you survived anything.

7

OLD FRIEND

Daphne arrived at seven with two bags of Chinese takeout and a smile that made Brianna's chest ache.

"Delivery for the distinguished Ms. Van Demir," she announced, sweeping past Brianna into the foyer. "And her extremely distinguished cat."

"Shrimp?" Mimi's thought cut through immediately, the Chartreux appearing at the edge of the living room with suspicious speed.

"Yes, Your Majesty, I brought your shrimp." Daphne set the bags on the kitchen counter and pulled out a small container, which she placed on Mimi's bench with exaggerated ceremony. "Steamed, not fried, light on the garlic, exactly as requested."

"Good human," Mimi thought, already eating.

Brianna leaned against the doorframe and watched them. Her oldest friend and her only friend, performing their familiar ritual. It should have been comforting. Instead, she felt the weight of everything she wasn't saying pressing down on her shoulders like a physical thing.

"You're staring," Daphne said, not looking up from unpacking the food.

"Just admiring the view."

"Flatterer." But she smiled, and tension loosened in Brianna's chest. "Grab plates. I got extra egg rolls because I know you pretend you don't want them and then steal half of mine."

They ate at the small table by the window, the way they'd done dozens of times before. Lo mein and kung pao chicken and the egg rolls Brianna definitely didn't want but somehow kept finding their way onto her plate. Daphne talked about her day.

"Endalyn from fourth period homeroom made her famous lemon shortbread again," Daphne said, stealing an egg roll. "Half the faculty showed up at her door by third period."

Brianna listened and nodded and made appropriate sounds, but her mind kept drifting. To Elijah's voice on the phone. To Marcus's hollow eyes. To the decision she still hadn't made, circling in her thoughts like a vulture waiting for something to die.

"Okay," Daphne said, setting down her chopsticks. "What's wrong?"

"Nothing's wrong."

"Bri." The nickname was gentle but firm. "I've known you for seven years. I can tell when you're not really here."

Seven years.

Brianna watched Daphne's hands as she unpacked the food—the way her fingers moved with that particular grace, the silver ring on her right hand catching the light. The same ring she'd been wearing the day they met.

The UNCC library. Late September, the air conditioning fighting a losing battle against North Carolina humidity. Brianna had been reaching for a book on medieval French poetry—research for a case involving forged manuscripts—when another hand had appeared beside hers. Warm brown skin against the faded spine.

"Either we're both incredibly pretentious," Daphne had said, "or this is fate."

Her laugh had startled Brianna. Open, unguarded, completely unselfconscious. The kind of laugh Brianna hadn't heard directed at her in decades. The librarian, Brenda Shields, whom Brianna had known for some years made a point to shush them. Brianna nodded her acquiescence.

Three hours of conversation. Coffee that went cold while they talked about Villon and Christine de Pizan and whether translation was betrayal or resurrection. Dinner at a Thai place where Daphne had ordered for both of them and somehow known exactly what Brianna would like. And then...

One night. One perfect, terrifying night when Brianna had let her guard down and let someone in and remembered, for a few hours, what it felt like to not be alone.

The next morning, she'd told Daphne everything. Sat across from her at the kitchen table, hands wrapped around a coffee mug for something to hold onto, and explained—calmly, thoroughly—exactly what Brianna was. What she'd done. What she could do. She'd watched Daphne's face for the flinch, the recoil, the dawning horror.

Instead, Daphne had tilted her head slightly. "So the not-eating-much thing at dinner—that's related?"

"I... yes."

"And you're how old, exactly?"

"Eight hundred and sixty-three. Give or take."

"Huh." Daphne had taken a sip of her own coffee, considering. "And here I thought the age gap with my last girlfriend was bad."

Brianna had stared at her. "You're not... you're not running."

"Should I be?"

"Most people would."

"I'm not most people." Daphne had set down her mug and reached across the table, her fingers brushing Brianna's wrist. "Okay. I have about four hundred more questions. But first—what do you want for breakfast?"

Seven years of friendship since that morning. Seven years of patience, of Daphne waiting for Brianna to be ready for something more. Seven years of Brianna keeping her at arm's length, close enough to need but never close enough to lose.

"Work stuff," Brianna said. "Complicated case."

"You've had complicated cases before. This is different." Daphne's dark eyes searched her face. "You look scared, Bri. I've never seen you look scared."

I am scared, Brianna thought. *More scared than I've been in two hundred years.*

But she couldn't say that. Couldn't explain about Elijah, about the choice she was facing, about all the ways her careful life was about to come crashing down. Daphne knew what Brianna was, but she didn't know about the Hierarchy. About Protectors. About the ancient monster who'd been watching Brianna for centuries and had finally decided to collect on his investment.

Telling her would mean dragging her into a world of violence and politics and dangers she couldn't possibly prepare for. It would mean putting a target on her back.

It would mean risking her the same way Garth had risked Brianna, all those centuries ago.

"I'm fine," she said. "Really. Just tired."

Daphne fell silent. Then she stood, gathered their empty plates, and carried them to the sink. Her movements were precise, controlled, the way they got when she was upset but trying not to show it.

"You know what I think about sometimes?" she said, her back to Brianna. "I think about how you look at me when you don't think I'm watching. Like I'm something precious. Something fragile." She turned, leaning against the counter, her arms crossed. "But I'm not fragile, Bri. I'm not some glass figurine you have to keep on a high shelf to protect."

"Daph—"

"I'm also not stupid. I know something's been different the last few days. You've been distant. Distracted. And now you're sitting across from me with that look in your eyes like you're already saying goodbye."

The words hit harder than they should have. Brianna opened her mouth to deny it, but nothing came out.

"Seven years," Daphne said. "I've been waiting for seven years. Waiting for you to trust me. Waiting for you to let me in. Waiting for you to stop treating me like I'm temporary." Her voice cracked slightly. "When are you going to let that be enough? When are you going to let me be enough?"

The question hung in the air between them, sharp and painful and impossible to answer.

Brianna thought about Garth. About the garden in Lyon where she'd first seen him, the way he'd looked at her like she was the most remarkable thing he'd ever encountered. About the eight years of happiness they'd shared before he'd left her alone with a grief that had never fully healed.

She'd made a promise after that. On a mountain in the Alps, with nothing but the wind and her own broken heart for company. She would never let anyone that close again. Would never put herself in a position to lose someone the way she'd lost him.

But here was Daphne, standing in her kitchen, asking for exactly what Brianna had sworn never to give.

"It's not about you being enough," Brianna said finally. "It's never been about that."

"Then what is it about?"

"It's about..." She stopped. Breathed. Tried to find words for something she'd never spoken aloud. "I had someone once. A long time ago. Before you, before any of this. He was... everything. And then one day he was gone. Just gone. No explanation, no goodbye, nothing. I spent decades looking for him. Centuries. I never found out what happened."

Daphne's expression softened slightly, but she didn't move from her position by the counter. "You told me about him. The first morning. You said his name was Garth."

"I didn't tell you everything." Brianna looked down at her hands, unable to meet Daphne's eyes. "I didn't tell you that losing him nearly destroyed me. That I spent years afterward barely surviving. That I made a promise to myself that I would never, never, let anyone close enough to hurt me like that again."

"Bri..."

"I look at you," Brianna continued, the words coming faster now, spilling out like water through a cracked dam, "and I see everything I could have. Everything I want. And then I imagine waking up one morning to find you gone, and I can't—I can't do it again. I can't survive that again."

"So instead, you'll just keep me at arm's length forever?" Daphne's voice was thick with frustration, with hurt, with seven years of waiting finally boiling over. "You'll just... what? Watch me grow old while you stay the same? Let me die eventually, knowing you never really let me in?"

"You wouldn't grow old." The words were out before Brianna could stop them.

Daphne went still. "What?"

Stupid, Brianna thought. Stupid, stupid, stupid.

"There's a way," she said slowly, carefully. "To make you like me. To give you... what I have. The years. The strength. All of it."

"Turning me." Daphne's voice was barely above a whisper. "You could turn me."

"I could. But I won't." Brianna forced herself to meet Daphne's eyes. "Because that would mean doing to you what was done to me. Taking your life, your humanity, your connection to the world you know. It would mean making you a target for everyone who hunts our kind. It would mean—"

"It would mean I could be with you forever."

The simplicity of it was devastating. Seven years of waiting, and this was what Daphne had been waiting for. Not just acceptance. Not just a relationship. But eternity.

"I made a promise," Brianna said. "After Garth. I swore I would never Birth another Valensi. Never take someone's humanity the way mine was taken. Never create a bond that could be broken the way ours was broken."

"Your promise isn't about protecting others, Bri. It's about protecting yourself." Daphne pushed off from the counter and crossed the kitchen, stopping just in front of Brianna's chair. "You're so afraid of losing someone again that you've decided not to have anyone at all. But that's not living. That's just... waiting to die."

"I can't die."

"Everyone dies eventually. Even your kind. Even the ones who've lived for a thousand years." Daphne reached out and took Brianna's hand. Her skin was warm, impossibly warm, alive in ways that Brianna hadn't been for eight centuries. "I'm not asking you to break your promise. Not tonight. I'm just asking you to stop pushing me away. To let me be here for whatever you're going through. To trust that I'm strong enough to handle it."

Brianna looked at their intertwined hands. Daphne's mocha skin against her own pale fingers, warmth against cold, mortality against eternity. Such a small thing. Such an enormous thing.

From the kitchen bench, Mimi watched them with ancient, knowing eyes.

"You're going to lose her eventually," the cat thought. "You know that."

I know, Brianna thought back.

"Then why are you wasting time?"

It was such a simple question. Such an obvious question. And Brianna, for all her centuries of wisdom, had no good answer.

"There are things happening," she said slowly, still holding Daphne's hand. "Dangerous things. Things I'm not sure I can protect you from."

"Then tell me about them. Let me help."

"I can't. Not yet. But soon." She squeezed Daphne's fingers gently. "I promise. Soon I'll tell you everything. And then you can decide if you still want to be here."

"I'll still want to be here." Daphne said it with absolute certainty. "I've wanted to be here since the moment I met you, Bri. That's not going to change."

Brianna wanted to believe her. Wanted it more than she'd wanted anything in centuries.

But belief was a luxury she couldn't afford. Not with Elijah's shadow looming over everything. Not with choices waiting to be made that could shatter both their lives.

"Stay tonight," she said instead. "Please."

Daphne's smile was like sunrise after a long, dark night. "I thought you'd never ask."

Later, after Daphne had fallen asleep beside her, Brianna lay awake and stared at the ceiling.

The warmth of Daphne's body was a comfort and a torment. Every breath, every small movement, was a reminder of what she stood to lose. What she was already losing, in a sense, by not being brave enough to truly let her in.

When are you going to let that be enough?

She thought about Lyon. About a garden filled with flowers and a young man who'd looked at her the way Daphne looked at her now—like she was worth waiting for. Worth risking everything for.

She'd let him in. She'd trusted him completely. And then she'd lost him so thoroughly that she didn't even know if he was alive or dead.

You're so afraid of losing someone again that you've decided not to have anyone at all.

Daphne was right. Of course she was right. But knowing something and doing something about it were very different things.

Brianna closed her eyes and tried not to think about the call she would have to make tomorrow. About Elijah waiting for her report. About the Hunter sitting in a jail cell, innocent of everything except trying to protect people from monsters.

About the choice that was bearing down on her like a freight train, and the lives that hung in the balance.

Tomorrow. She would deal with it tomorrow.

Tonight, she would let herself have this one small thing. This warmth. This presence. This woman who loved her despite everything, or maybe because of it.

Tonight, she would pretend that she deserved to be happy.

8

THE GARDEN

Lyon, 1150

The garden was Basina's sanctuary.

She knelt in the dirt between rows of herbs, her hands buried in the dark soil, utterly content. The falling summer sun warmed her back through the linen of her dress, and the air smelled of rosemary and lavender and the particular green sweetness of things growing. Her mother despaired of her. A merchant's daughter should not spend her days crawling in the dirt like a peasant. But Basina had long since stopped caring what a merchant's daughter should or should not do.

The garden was hers. She had planted every seed, tended every sprout, coaxed life from the earth with patience and care. When everything else in her life felt uncertain. Her father's moods, her mother's expectations, the parade of suitors who looked at her like a ledger to be balanced. She could come here and remember that some things grew simply because you loved them enough to try.

She was sixteen years old, and she had already learned that love was the rarest thing in the world.

Even as the sun dipped below the horizon, a shadow fell across the herbs.

"You have a gift."

Basina looked up, peering against the early evening light. A man stood at the edge of the garden path. Perhaps thirty years old, well-dressed in the manner of a traveling merchant, with dark hair and eyes that seemed to hold more years than his face suggested. He was watching her with an expression she couldn't quite read. Interest, certainly. But something else beneath it. Something patient and careful and very still.

"I beg your pardon?" she said.

"Your garden." He gestured at the neat rows of herbs, the climbing roses along the stone wall, the riot of color and life that surrounded her. "It's remarkable. Most gardens I've seen are functional. This one is... loved."

She should have been alarmed. A strange man in her family's garden, appearing without announcement, speaking to her without introduction. Her mother would have had fits. Her father would have called for the servants.

But something in his manner put her at ease. He wasn't leering at her the way the young men at market did. Wasn't calculating her worth the way her father's business partners did when they thought she wasn't watching. He was simply... observing. Like someone who had stumbled upon something beautiful and wanted to appreciate it properly.

"Thank you," she said, and returned to her weeding. "Most people don't notice gardens at all."

"Most people don't notice much of anything." He moved closer, his footsteps quiet on the packed earth path. "May I?"

She glanced up again. He was gesturing to a stone bench near the rose trellis, asking permission to sit. In her garden. Like a guest requesting hospitality rather than a stranger presuming upon it.

"If you like," she said.

He sat, arranging himself with a peculiar grace, and watched her work in silence. It should have been uncomfortable. This unknown man studying her as she crawled in the dirt. But somehow it wasn't. The silence between them felt natural. Unforced. Like the pause between one breath and the next.

"You're not from Lyon," she said eventually.

"No. I travel a great deal. Business interests in various cities."

"What sort of business?"

"The tedious kind. Contracts and negotiations and men who talk too much about money." He smiled slightly, and something in Basina's chest responded to it despite herself. "I find gardens far more interesting."

"Most men find gardens boring."

"Most men are fools."

She laughed. A startled, genuine sound that escaped before she could stop it. He seemed pleased by this, though he didn't show it in any obvious way. Just a slight softening around his eyes, a warmth that hadn't been there a moment before.

"I'm Garth," he said. "Garth Van Demir."

"Basina Courtois."

"A pleasure, Basina Courtois." He said her name carefully, like he was committing it to memory. "I apologize for intruding on your sanctuary. I was walking past your family's house and saw the flowers over the wall. I couldn't resist investigating."

"You climbed our wall?"

"The gate was open." He gestured toward the garden entrance, which was indeed standing ajar. "Though I admit I might have climbed if it hadn't been."

"That's very forward of you."

"So I've been told." He leaned back on the bench, tilting his face toward the darkening sky with an expression of quiet pleasure. "I've found that the most interesting things in life rarely happen to those who follow all the rules."

Basina considered this. Her mother would say it was the philosophy of scoundrels and thieves. Her father would say it was the excuse of men who couldn't succeed through honest means.

But something about the way Garth said it, without bravado, without self-congratulation, just a simple statement of observed truth—made her think he might be right.

"What's the most interesting thing you've ever found?" she asked. "By not following the rules?"

He turned his head to look at her, and for just a moment, something ancient flickered in his eyes. Something that made her think of deep water and old forests and the patient turning of seasons beyond counting.

"I'm not sure yet," he said. "I might be looking at it."

He came back the next day.

And the day after that.

Basina found herself listening for his footsteps on the garden path, her heart quickening at the creak of the gate. They talked about everything and nothing. About plants and poetry, about the world beyond Lyon's walls, about the small observations that made up a life. He asked questions that no one had ever thought to ask her. What did she dream about? What made her angry? What would she do if she could do anything at all?

She told him things she'd never told anyone. About the loneliness of being an only child in a house full of servants. About her mother's disappointment that she wasn't more feminine, more tractable, more interested in the suitors who came calling with their ledgers and their expectations. About the way she sometimes felt like she was waiting for her real life to begin, marking time until something—she didn't know what—finally happened.

He listened like every word mattered. Like she mattered.

"You're very patient," she said one afternoon, three weeks into whatever this was becoming. "Most men would have tried to kiss me by now."

"Would you like me to try?"

Her face flushed hot. "That's not what I meant."

"I know." He was smiling, but there was no mockery in it. "You meant that most men pursue what they want without much thought for what the other person wants. They see something they desire and they reach for it, like children grabbing sweets."

"And you're not like that?"

"I've learned to be more careful." His expression shifted. A shadow passing behind his eyes, there and gone so quickly she almost missed it. "I've learned that the things worth having are worth waiting for. Worth doing properly."

"Properly?"

"When you plant a garden," he said, gesturing at the roses climbing the wall, "you don't expect flowers the first day. You prepare the soil. You choose the right seeds. You water and tend and wait, because you understand that growth takes time." He met her eyes, and the weight of his gaze made her breath catch. "The best things in life are the same. They can't be rushed. They can only be cultivated."

Basina didn't know what to say to that. Didn't know what to do with the feeling building in her chest. Something warm and terrifying and entirely new.

"My father will want to know your intentions," she said finally. "If you keep visiting."

"Then perhaps I should speak with him."

"You want to speak with my father?"

"I want to do this properly." He stood, brushing dust from his traveling clothes, and offered her his hand to help her rise. His grip was firm and steady, and she found she didn't want to let go. "If you'll permit me to call on your family formally, I would be honored."

She stared at him. At this strange, patient man who had appeared in her garden and somehow become the most important thing in her small world.

"I don't even know you," she said. "Not really. I don't know where you come from, or who your family is, or—"

"Ask me anything."

"Anything?"

"I'll answer honestly. Whatever you want to know."

There were a thousand questions she should have asked. About his business, his background, his family name that she'd never heard in any of the merchant circles her father traveled. About where he went when he left her garden, where he stayed at night, why a man of obvious means was spending his evenings talking to a merchant's daughter in the dirt.

Instead, she asked: "Why me?"

It was the question that had been burning in her since the first day. Why her, out of all the women in Lyon? Why this garden, this house, this particular unremarkable girl with dirt under her fingernails and dreams she couldn't name?

Garth was silent for a beat. When he finally spoke, his voice was different. Softer, more serious, stripped of the easy charm he usually wore.

"Because you're the first person in a very long time who made me want to stop."

"Stop what?"

"Moving. Running. Whatever you want to call it." He still held her hand, his thumb tracing small circles against her palm. "I've been traveling for longer than you can imagine, Basina. I've seen cities rise and fall. I've watched generations live and die. And somewhere along the way, I forgot what it felt like to want something for myself. To see something beautiful and think: this, this is worth staying for."

She should have been confused by his words. Should have questioned what he meant by generations, by cities rising and falling, by a lifetime of travel that seemed too vast for his thirty years.

But standing there in the golden afternoon light, with his hand in hers and his eyes holding truths she couldn't quite comprehend, all she felt was certainty.

"Come back tomorrow," she said. "I'll introduce you to my father."

His smile was like sunrise after a long, dark night.

"I would like that very much. Unfortunately, I won't be available until just after dusk. I hope that is suitable." She only nodded.

He released her hand and walked to the garden gate, pausing at the threshold to look back at her. She was still standing among the roses, dirt on her dress, her heart pounding with something that felt like the beginning of everything.

"Until tomorrow, Basina Courtois."

"Until tomorrow."

He left, and she stood in her garden for a long time afterward, watching the moonlight fall over her garden and wondering how her whole world had shifted without her noticing.

She didn't know, then, what he was. Didn't understand the weight of what he was offering, or the centuries that stretched out before them like an unwritten book.

She only knew that she had been waiting for something, and it had finally arrived.

8

RESIGNATION

Brianna left Daphne sleeping and arrived at the office before seven.

The building was quiet at this hour. Just the security guards and the cleaning crew finishing their rounds. She liked it this way. The stillness before the storm, the brief window of peace before the phones started ringing and the machinery of justice ground back into motion.

She made coffee in the break room and carried it to her desk, staring at the stack of files waiting for her attention. The Ross case sat on top, exactly where she'd left it yesterday. She hadn't opened it again. Hadn't needed to. Marcus's words were still echoing in her head, mixing with Elijah's voice, with Daphne's questions, with the weight of decisions she still hadn't made.

I expect you'll have something useful to share by then.

Today. He'd said he would call today.

She picked up the Ross file and flipped it open, scanning the arrest report one more time. John Sebastian Ross. Thirty-two years old. Military veteran. Currently employed by Madronite Industries.

She still hadn't looked into Madronite. Part of her didn't want to know. As long as she remained ignorant, she could pretend this was just a normal case. A straightforward assault charge. Nothing that required her to choose between her conscience and her survival.

But she was done pretending.

She pulled up a browser on her computer and typed in the company name.

Madronite Industries. Founded 2001. Headquarters in Charlotte, North Carolina. Primary business: high-end furniture and construction materials made from a proprietary composite called Madronite. CEO and founder: Matthew DiBondra.

It looked legitimate. Boring, even. The kind of company that made products nobody thought about until they needed them.

But Brianna had lived long enough to know that the most dangerous things often wore the most mundane disguises.

She dug deeper. Press releases. Business filings. The occasional news article about charitable donations and community involvement. Everything squeaky clean. Everything exactly what you'd expect from a successful mid-sized manufacturing company.

Too clean, maybe.

She was about to give up when she found a small mention in a trade publication from 2008. A brief article about Madronite's expansion into "specialized security applications." No details. No follow-up. Just a single paragraph buried in a roundup of industry news.

Specialized security applications.

She thought about Ross's military background. About the knife that had turned a Valensi to ash. About the word "Hawthorn" that Marcus had mentioned in passing. Something Ross had muttered while fighting the Baneful, a name that meant nothing to the boy but had sent a chill down Brianna's spine.

She'd heard whispers, over the centuries. Rumors of humans who knew about the Valensi. Who hunted them. Who had developed weapons and tactics specifically designed to kill creatures that most people didn't believe existed.

She'd always dismissed those rumors as paranoid fantasies. Humans were cattle, the Hierarchy said. Prey animals who occasionally got lucky. The idea that they could organize, could develop technology to threaten the Valensi, was laughable.

But here was a company that made materials capable of killing her kind. Here was a man who worked for that company, who carried their weapons, who had used them to turn a Baneful to ash in a Charlotte alley.

Here was proof that the rumors were true.

"You're in early."

Brianna looked up. Mark was standing in the doorway, coffee in hand, eyebrows raised in surprise.

"Couldn't sleep," she said, closing the browser window. "You?"

"Pre-trial prep for the Henderson case. Jury selection starts tomorrow." He dropped into his chair and began shuffling through papers. "You okay? You look... tired."

"I'm fine."

"If you say so." He didn't sound convinced, but he let it drop. That was one of the things she appreciated about Mark. He knew when not to push.

The office filled up gradually as the morning progressed. Julie arrived with her usual efficiency, distributing files and fielding phone calls. The other ADAs trickled in, bringing with them the low hum of conversation and the click of keyboards. Normalcy. Routine. The comfortable rhythms of a life Brianna had built over the past decade.

A life that was about to end.

The meeting with Oscar Ricemen was scheduled for ten o'clock.

Brianna had requested it the previous afternoon, citing a "personnel matter" she needed to discuss. Oscar had agreed without asking questions. He trusted her judgment, had trusted it for years. She was his best prosecutor, his most reliable team lead, the one he turned to when cases got complicated.

He had no idea what she was about to do.

She found him in his office, reviewing documents with the distracted intensity of a man with too much on his plate. He was in his sixties now, silver-haired and slightly stooped, with the weary eyes of someone who'd spent decades fighting battles he couldn't always win.

She'd liked him from the beginning. Respected him. He was one of the few genuinely good men she'd met in her centuries of existence.

Leaving him was going to hurt.

"Brianna." He looked up and smiled. "Close the door. What's on your mind?"

She closed the door and sat in the chair across from his desk. For a moment, she didn't speak. Just looked at him. At this man who'd given her a chance, who'd championed her work, who'd never once questioned why a woman with no verifiable history before 2010 was so remarkably good at her job.

"I need to resign," she said.

The smile faded. "I'm sorry?"

"Effective immediately. I know it's sudden, and I know it leaves you in a difficult position, but I don't have a choice."

Oscar leaned back in his chair, studying her with the sharp assessment that had made him such an effective prosecutor in his own day. "What's going on, Brianna? Are you in some kind of trouble?"

"No. Nothing like that." The lie came easily. She'd had centuries of practice. "It's a personal matter. Family emergency. I need to deal with it, and I can't do that while maintaining my responsibilities here."

"Family." He said the word carefully. "I didn't know you had family."

"Distant relatives. Out of state. It's complicated."

"Most things are." He was quiet for a long moment, his fingers steepled beneath his chin. "You know I can't just let you walk away. You're in the middle of a dozen active cases. The Henderson trial starts next week. The—"

"Mark can handle Henderson. He's ready." She kept her voice steady, professional. "I've prepared transition notes for all my active files. Julie can distribute them to the team this afternoon."

"You've prepared transition notes." His eyebrows rose. "This isn't sudden at all, is it? You've been planning this."

Not planning, she thought. Just... prepared. Always prepared.

"I'm sorry, Oscar. I know this is unfair to you. To everyone. But I don't have a choice."

He studied her, and she could see him weighing his options. He could refuse. Could make her work out a notice period, could tie her up in HR procedures and exit interviews and all the machinery of institutional departure. He had that power.

But Oscar Ricemen hadn't become District Attorney by failing to read people.

"You're not coming back," he said. It wasn't a question.

"No. I'm not."

"And you're not going to tell me what this is really about."

"I can't."

He sighed. A deep, weary sound that seemed to come from somewhere far down in his chest. "I've worked with a lot of prosecutors over the years, Brianna. Some of them were talented. Some of them were dedicated. A few of them were even genuinely good people." He met her eyes. "You're all three. And you're also the most mysterious person I've ever met. No history, no connections, no past that anyone can verify. It's like you appeared out of thin air ten years ago, fully formed and ready to work."

She didn't respond. There was nothing to say.

"I'm not going to ask what you're running from," he continued. "That's your business. But whatever it is, I hope you find what you're looking for." He stood and extended his hand. "It's been an honor working with you."

She shook his hand, feeling the warmth of his grip, the genuine respect in his eyes. This man would be dead in twenty years, maybe thirty. She would still be walking the earth, wearing another name, building another life. And she would remember this moment—this small, human kindness—for centuries after he was gone.

"Thank you, Oscar. For everything."

"Take care of yourself, Brianna. Whatever that means for you."

She left his office and didn't look back.

Cleaning out her desk took less than an hour.

There wasn't much to take. A few personal items. A photograph of Mimi, a small plant that Julie had given her for her "birthday" three years ago, a coffee mug with a faded quote about justice. The detritus of a decade, easily packed into a single cardboard box.

Mark watched her from across the room, his expression troubled. Julie had tears in her eyes, though she was trying to hide them. The other ADAs murmured among themselves, confused and concerned and already speculating about what had happened.

Let them speculate. By next week, they'd have moved on. A new prosecutor would take her office. The cases would be reassigned. The machinery would keep grinding forward.

That was the thing about human lives. They were so brief, so easily disrupted, so quick to heal and forget. Brianna had seen it happen a hundred times. A thousand. People mourned, and then they moved on, and eventually even the mourning faded into weary acceptance.

She would be a story they told at happy hours. Remember Van Demir? Whatever happened to her? And then even the stories would fade, and she would be nothing but a name on old case files, a ghost in institutional memory.

It was easier that way. It had to be.

"Brianna." Mark intercepted her at the elevator, his face earnest and worried. "Whatever's going on—if you need help, if there's anything—"

"I'm fine, Mark." She managed a smile. "You're going to be great. Oscar's going to lean on you hard for the next few months, but you're ready. Trust yourself."

"That's not—I'm not worried about the cases. I'm worried about you."

The sincerity in his voice made her chest ache. Such a simple thing, human concern. Such a rare thing, in her experience.

"I know," she said. "And I appreciate it. More than you know."

The elevator arrived. She stepped inside, box in her arms, and turned to face him.

"Take care of Julie," she said. "She's going to take this hard."

The doors closed before he could respond.

She sat in her car in the parking garage for a long time, the box on the passenger seat beside her.

The sun was streaming through the windshield, warm on her face. She'd spent a century burning in that light, teaching her body to accept what should have destroyed it. Now she sat in it without flinching, a Solari among shadows, a creature of daylight in a world that expected her to hide.

Time to become the District Attorney again, she'd thought yesterday morning. Time to pretend.

She wasn't pretending anymore.

The phone in her pocket buzzed. Unknown number. She knew who it was before she answered.

"Brianna." Elijah's voice was warm, almost friendly. "I trust you have something to report?"

She looked at the sunlight on her hands. At the life she'd just walked away from. At the future stretching out before her, uncertain and terrifying and entirely her own.

"We need to meet," she said. "In person."

A pause. Then, with evident pleasure: "How delightful. I'll send you the details."

The line went dead.

Brianna sat in the light and waited for the darkness to come.

10

RECKONING

Daphne was waiting on the porch when Brianna pulled into the driveway.

That was the first warning sign. Daphne had a key. Had been given one two years ago, after one too many evenings waiting in her car for Brianna to get home from late court sessions. She never waited outside unless something was wrong.

The second warning sign was her posture. Arms crossed. Shoulders tight. The coiled tension of someone holding back an explosion through sheer force of will.

Brianna parked and sat for a moment, gathering herself. She'd known this was coming. Had known it from the moment she'd walked out of Oscar's office. Word traveled fast in the legal community, and Daphne had friends at the courthouse. Clerks and paralegals who would have heard the news within hours.

She got out of the car, leaving the box of desk items on the passenger seat, and walked up the path to face what was coming.

"You quit." Daphne's voice was flat, controlled. The voice she used when she was too angry for volume. "You quit your job, and you didn't even tell me."

"Daph—"

"I had to hear it from Mariana in the clerk's office. She called to ask if you were okay. If I was okay. Because apparently my girlfriend, or whatever the hell you are, just walked out of a decade-long career without any warning, and I didn't even know it happened."

"I was going to tell you tonight."

"Tonight." Daphne laughed. A harsh, brittle sound. "After the fact. After you'd already made the decision, already cleaned out your desk, already walked away from everything. You were going to inform me. Like I'm some casual acquaintance who gets the news after everyone else."

Brianna didn't have an answer for that. It was true. All of it was true.

"Can we go inside?" she asked. "Please. I'll explain everything."

"You've been saying that for two days. 'Soon.' 'I'll tell you everything.' But you never do, Bri. You just keep pushing me away and expecting me to accept it."

"I know. And I'm sorry. But this." She gestured vaguely at the porch, the street, the neighbors who might be watching. "This isn't a conversation we should have out here."

Something in her tone must have registered, because Daphne's expression shifted slightly. The anger was still there, but beneath it now was something else. Fear.

"Fine," she said. "Inside. But you're going to tell me the truth this time. The real truth. All of it."

Brianna nodded and unlocked the door.

Mimi was curled on the back of the sofa, watching them with knowing, knowing eyes.

"Bad?" she thought at Brianna.

Very.

"Good luck."

Brianna almost laughed. Almost. Instead, she walked to the kitchen and poured two glasses of wine without asking if Daphne wanted one. Her hands were shaking slightly. She couldn't remember the last time her hands had shaken.

Daphne stood in the living room doorway, still radiating tension, but she accepted the glass when Brianna offered it. A small concession. A willingness to listen, at least for now.

"Sit," Brianna said. "Please."

They sat. Brianna in the armchair by the window, Daphne on the edge of the sofa, as far from relaxed as a person could be while technically seated. The silence stretched between them, heavy with everything that was about to change.

"I quit because I had to," Brianna said finally. "Not because I wanted to. Because something happened, something I can't control, and I can't be that person anymore. The ADA. The professional. The woman with the normal life."

"What happened?"

"Someone found me." The words came out rougher than she'd intended. "Someone from my past. Someone I've been running from for a very long time."

Daphne's brow furrowed. "Running from? Bri, you're eight hundred years old. Who could you possibly be running from?"

"His name is Elijah." Just saying it out loud made her chest tighten. "He's a Protector. One of the enforcers for the Valensi Hierarchy. The governing body of my kind. And he's... he's not like me. He's not like anyone you've ever met."

"What does he want?"

"Right now? He wants me to help him find someone. A human. A Hunter who's been killing Valensi in Charlotte." She took a long sip of wine, buying time. "The man I told you about. Ross. The one in my case file. He's the target."

"And you're supposed to hand him over?"

"Yes."

"Are you going to?"

Brianna looked at her. At this woman who had waited seven years, who had loved without condition, who deserved so much better than the half-truths and evasions Brianna had been feeding her.

"No," she said. "I'm not. Ross saved a boy's life. He's killing the ones who hurt people, the ones who hunt for pleasure. He's not a murderer. And Elijah..." She trailed off, the memories rising unbidden. The townhouse. The paralysis. The promises whispered in the dark. "Elijah is a monster. The real kind. The kind that wears a charming face and enjoys causing pain."

"You've met him before."

"Once. A long time ago." Her voice had gone flat, distant. "He found me in London. In 1799. I thought I'd escaped him. Thought if I hid well enough, stayed hidden long enough, he'd forget about me." She laughed bitterly. "He didn't forget. He never forgets."

Daphne was silent for a long moment, processing. When she spoke again, her voice was softer, the anger giving way to something more complicated.

"What happened in London?"

"I don't want to talk about London."

"Bri—"

"I can't talk about London. Not yet. Maybe not ever." Brianna set down her wine glass before she shattered it. "But I can tell you why I am the way I am. Why I keep everyone at a distance. Why I made that promise about never Birthing anyone." She met Daphne's eyes. "I can tell you about Garth."

The name hung in the air between them. Daphne had heard it before—that first morning, when Brianna had laid out the basic facts of her existence. A husband. Long ago. Gone now. That was all she'd offered then.

It wasn't going to be enough anymore.

"Tell me," Daphne said.

So Brianna told her.

"I was sixteen when I met him."

She started with the garden. With the summer evening light and the smell of lavender and the shadow falling across the herbs. With a man who appeared at the edge of the path and said, You have a gift.

"He was different from anyone I'd ever known. Patient. Interested in what I thought, what I felt, what I dreamed about. He didn't treat me like a prize to be won or a problem to be solved. He treated me like a person."

She told Daphne about the courtship. The evening visits, because he could only come after dark. The conversations that lasted for hours, covering everything and nothing. The way he'd asked her father's permission to court her formally, had provided a dowry that raised no suspicions despite coming from mysterious origins.

"He told me what he was on our wedding night. After the ceremony, after everything was official and binding. He sat me down and explained—what he was, what the Birthing meant, what I would become if I chose it." She paused, remembering. "He gave me a choice. A real choice. He said he would walk away if that's what I wanted. That he would rather lose me than take my humanity without my full understanding and consent."

"But you chose him."

"I chose forever." Brianna's voice cracked slightly. "I was eighteen years old and I chose to spend eternity with the man I loved. And for eight years, it was everything he promised. We traveled. We built lives together. We were happy."

"And then?"

"And then he disappeared."

The words came out flat, matter-of-fact, stripped of the eight centuries of anguish they represented.

"One autumn morning in 1160, he left our cottage to arrange our next relocation. We moved constantly, to stay ahead of anyone who might notice we didn't age. He said he'd be back by nightfall." She stared at her hands, at the fingers that still remembered the shape of his face. "He never came back."

Daphne didn't say anything. Just waited, giving Brianna the space to continue.

"I searched for decades. Centuries. Every rumor, every whisper, every contact we'd ever made. I followed them all. Nothing. It was like he'd simply ceased to exist. No body. No message. No explanation." She looked up, and her eyes were dry but burning. "Do you know what that's like? To love someone that completely and then have them vanish? To spend centuries not knowing if they're dead or alive, if they left by choice or were taken, if they're out there somewhere thinking about you the way you're thinking about them?"

"No," Daphne said softly. "I can't imagine."

"I went to the mountains after. The Alps. I stayed there for two years, alone, trying to decide if I wanted to keep existing. In the end, I made three promises to myself. I would never Birth another Valensi. I would never kill another person. And I would never let anyone get close enough to hurt me like that again."

She reached for her wine, found the glass empty, set it back down.

"For centuries, I've kept those promises. I've built lives and abandoned them. I've watched people age and die while I stayed the same. I've kept everyone at arm's length. Colleagues, acquaintances, anyone who might become something more. Because I couldn't bear to lose someone like that again. I couldn't survive it a second time."

"And then you met me."

"And then I met you." Brianna's voice softened. "And you were so stubborn. So patient. You wouldn't let me push you away. You kept showing up, kept asking questions, kept looking at me like I was worth waiting for."

"You are worth waiting for."

"I'm a broken woman, Daphne. I'm eight centuries of grief wearing a human face. I've done things I'm not proud of. I've run from fights I should have faced. I've let fear dictate every major decision of my existence."

"And yet here you are." Daphne set down her wine glass and moved to kneel in front of Brianna's chair, taking her hands. "You quit your job. You told Elijah you want to meet in person. You're not running this time. Why?"

Brianna looked at their intertwined fingers. Daphne's warmth against her own, two lives tangled together despite everything she'd done to prevent it.

"Because I'm tired," she said. "I'm tired of hiding. I'm tired of being afraid. And I'm tired of pushing away the one person who's made me feel alive in eight hundred years." She squeezed Daphne's hands. "I can't promise you forever. I can't promise that I'll survive whatever's coming. But I can promise that I'm done running. Whatever happens next, I'm going to face it. And I want you beside me when I do."

Daphne was crying. Brianna hadn't noticed when it started—the tears were sliding silently down her cheeks, catching the lamplight.

"That's all I've ever wanted," she said. "Just to be beside you. Whatever that means. However long we have."

Brianna pulled her up from the floor, into her lap, into her arms. Held her the way she'd been afraid to hold anyone for centuries. Let herself feel the warmth and the weight and the terrifying, exhilarating reality of someone who loved her despite everything.

"I'm scared," she admitted, the words muffled against Daphne's hair.

"I know. Me too."

"This might end badly. For both of us."

"I know that too."

"And you're still here."

Daphne pulled back just far enough to look at her, those dark eyes fierce with certainty.

"I'm still here. I'm always going to be here. That's what love is, Bri. Showing up even when it's terrifying. Especially when it's terrifying."

Brianna kissed her then. Not with the careful restraint of the past seven years, but with everything she'd been holding back. All the fear and the longing and the desperate, fragile hope that maybe, just maybe, she didn't have to be alone anymore.

When they finally broke apart, Daphne was smiling through her tears.

"So," she said. "What's the plan?"

Brianna laughed. A real laugh, surprising even herself.

"I have absolutely no idea."

"Then we'll figure it out together."

Together. Such a simple word. Such a terrifying, beautiful word.

For the first time in centuries, Brianna let herself believe it might be true.

11

FALLING

Garth Van Demir had lived for nine hundred years, and he had learned many things in that time.

He had learned that empires rose and fell like tides. That languages shifted and mutated, that borders were drawn and redrawn, that the humans who dominated this world lived their brief lives in a constant state of reinvention. He had watched Rome crumble. Had seen the Franks carve kingdoms from the wreckage. Had walked through the chaos of centuries and emerged unchanged, untouched, eternal.

He had learned that eternity was a burden as much as a gift. That watching everyone around you age and die while you remained the same hollowed something out inside you, left you numb to the small joys that made mortal lives bearable. He had stopped counting the years sometime around his fifth century. What was the point? The years would keep coming whether he counted them or not.

He had learned caution. To build lives that could be abandoned, connections that could be severed, identities that could be shed like old skin. The Hierarchy had rules about these things. About how long a Valensi could stay in one place, about the dangers of forming attachments, about the absolute prohibition against Birthing without permission. He had followed those rules for centuries. They kept him safe. They kept everyone safe.

And then he had seen a girl kneeling in a garden, her hands buried in the soil, utterly absorbed in the simple act of making things grow.

And everything he had learned in nine hundred years had suddenly seemed very far away.

The courtship was unlike anything Garth had experienced before.

In his youth, his true youth, in the years before his Birthing, courtship had been a transaction. Families negotiating. Dowries exchanged. Love, if it came at all, came later, after the contracts were signed and the marriages consummated. He had been Birthed before he'd had the chance to experience any of that, pulled from his mortal life by a Valensi who had seen potential in a Roman soldier and hadn't bothered asking permission.

In the centuries since, he had taken lovers. Brief encounters, mostly. Physical needs met with willing partners who never knew what he really was. He had told himself it was enough. Had convinced himself that the emptiness afterward was simply the price of immortality.

Basina was different.

She didn't want his body. Or rather, she did, but that wasn't what drew her to him. She wanted his attention. His thoughts. His stories about the world beyond Lyon's walls. She asked questions that no one had asked him in centuries, questions that made him remember what it felt like to be genuinely known.

And she made him laugh. God help him, she made him laugh in ways he hadn't laughed since before his Birthing.

"You're very old, aren't you?" she asked one evening, three months into whatever this was becoming.

They were sitting in her garden, their garden now, in some unspoken way, watching the last light fade from the sky. He could only visit after sunset, a limitation he'd explained away with vague references to business obligations and sensitive skin. She'd accepted the excuse without question, though he sometimes caught her watching him with those thoughtful eyes, piecing together clues she didn't yet have context for.

"What makes you say that?" he asked carefully.

"The way you talk about things. Places. Events." She tilted her head, studying him. "Last week you mentioned the sack of Rome like you'd been there. Like you'd seen it happen."

He should have been more careful. Should have watched his words more closely. But something about her made him careless, made him forget the centuries of caution that had kept him alive.

"I read a great deal," he said. "History has always fascinated me."

"Mmm." She didn't sound convinced. "And the way you move. The way you're always listening for things I can't hear. The way you never eat when we're together, even though I've offered you food a dozen times."

"I eat before I come. I wouldn't want to impose on your family's hospitality."

"Garth." Her voice was gentle but firm. "I'm not stupid. I know there's something you're not telling me. I've known it since the first day."

He was quiet for a long moment. The twilight was deepening around them, the first stars emerging in the darkening sky. Somewhere in the house, he could hear her mother moving around, preparing the evening meal. Normal sounds. Human sounds. The soundtrack of a world he'd been observing from the outside for nearly a millennium.

"If I told you," he said finally, "you might not want me to come back."

"Then I'd be a fool." She reached out and took his hand—bold for a young woman of her time, scandalous by the standards of her class. "I've spent my whole life waiting for something I couldn't name. And then you appeared in my garden, and suddenly I knew what it was. I was waiting for you. Whatever you are, whoever you are, I was waiting for you."

He should have told her then. Should have confessed everything, given her the full truth and let her make an informed choice. That was what the honorable path demanded.

But he was afraid. For the first time in centuries, he was genuinely afraid. Not of death or danger, but of losing something precious. Of watching her face change when she learned what he was. Of seeing disgust or fear or betrayal in those remarkable eyes.

"Soon," he said. "I'll tell you everything soon. But not yet. Please. Give me a little more time."

She studied him, then nodded.

"I'll wait," she said. "I've been waiting sixteen years for my life to begin. I can wait a little longer."

He met her father three weeks later.

Henri Courtois was a successful merchant. Textiles, mostly, with some trade in spices from the East. He was shrewd, practical, and deeply suspicious of the well-dressed stranger who had been spending evenings in his garden with his only daughter.

"You say you're a merchant yourself," Henri said, eyeing Garth across the dinner table. Garth had finally accepted an invitation to join the family for their evening meal. A necessary step if he wanted to pursue this courtship formally. "Yet I've never heard your name in any of the trading circles. No one seems to know where you come from or who your family is."

"I deal primarily in the German territories," Garth replied smoothly. "Precious metals. Gems, occasionally. My business takes me far from Lyon, which is why I'm not well known here."

"And yet you've been in Lyon for months now. Visiting my daughter every evening." Henri's eyes narrowed. "What exactly are your intentions, Monsieur Van Demir?"

Garth set down his wine glass and met the older man's gaze directly.

"I intend to marry her," he said. "With your permission, of course. I intend to provide for her, to protect her, to give her a life of comfort and security. I intend to love her for as long as I live."

The words were true. All of them. He just didn't mention how long that might be.

Henri studied him. The kind of assessment a man made when evaluating a business partner. Weighing costs and benefits. Calculating risks.

"You're older than you look," he said finally.

Garth felt his pulse quicken. "What makes you say that?"

"The way you carry yourself. The way you speak. You have the manner of a man who's seen a great deal of the world." Henri leaned back in his chair. "I was young once. I thought I knew everything. You don't have that arrogance. You have the patience of someone who's learned that time moves slowly and the world doesn't change as fast as we'd like."

"I've traveled extensively," Garth said carefully. "It teaches perspective."

"I imagine it does." Henri was quiet for a moment, then inclined his head. "I'll be honest with you, Monsieur Van Demir. My daughter is... unusual. She's intelligent, which is inconvenient in a woman. She's stubborn, which is worse. She has opinions about things no woman of her station should have opinions about, and she's not shy about expressing them."

"Those are among her finest qualities."

Henri's eyebrows rose. "Most men would consider them defects."

"Most men are fools."

A surprised laugh escaped the merchant. The same kind of startled sound that Basina made when Garth said something unexpected. The family resemblance was suddenly, sharply apparent.

"She said you were different," Henri admitted. "I'm beginning to see what she meant." He reached for his wine. "Very well. You may court her formally. But I want a proper dowry negotiation. I want contracts. I want to know that my daughter will be provided for."

"I'll provide whatever you require."

"We'll see about that." But Henri was smiling now, the suspicion in his eyes replaced by something closer to respect. "Welcome to the family, Monsieur Van Demir. Such as it is."

The wedding was held in the spring of 1152.

It was a small ceremony. Basina's family, a few trusted friends, a priest who asked no questions about the groom's mysterious background. Garth had provided a dowry that far exceeded what was customary, enough to silence any lingering doubts Henri might have had about his new son-in-law's financial situation.

The money was easy. Garth had accumulated wealth over nine centuries, hidden in various forms across a dozen countries. What was harder was the knowledge of what came next.

He had to tell her.

The Hierarchy's laws were clear. Birthing without permission was forbidden. One of the few offenses that carried a death sentence for both the creator and the created. But those laws existed to prevent reckless Birthings, to stop Valensi from turning humans on a whim and creating problems for everyone. They weren't meant to prevent this—a genuine love, a genuine choice, a woman who deserved to know the truth before she committed her life to a creature of the night.

At least, that's what Garth told himself.

The wedding feast lasted until well into the night. Garth sat beside his new bride, watching her laugh with her parents, watching the candlelight play across her features, and felt something that might have been joy if it hadn't been so thoroughly tangled with terror.

He was about to change her life forever. About to take everything she knew and burn it to ash. About to offer her an eternity that most humans couldn't even comprehend, let alone accept.

And if she said no, if she looked at him with horror instead of love, he would have to walk away. Would have to leave her with the knowledge of what existed in the shadows, the awareness that monsters were real and one of them had almost claimed her for his own.

He couldn't do that to her. Couldn't shatter her world and then abandon her to pick up the pieces alone.

Which meant she had to say yes. She had to.

And if she didn't?

He didn't know. For the first time in nine hundred years, Garth Van Demir genuinely didn't know what he would do.

The cottage they'd taken for their wedding night was small but comfortable. A stone building on the outskirts of Lyon, far enough from the city that they wouldn't be disturbed. Garth had arranged it specifically for this moment. For this conversation.

Basina stood by the window, still in her wedding dress, watching the moon rise over the hills. She was beautiful in the silver light—young and alive and impossibly precious.

"You're nervous," she said without turning around. "I can feel it."

"Can you?"

"You've been tense all evening. Through the feast, the dancing, the farewells. You barely touched your wine." She turned to face him. "Whatever it is you've been waiting to tell me, this is the moment, isn't it?"

He nodded slowly. "Yes. This is the moment."

"Then tell me." She crossed the room and took his hands in hers. "Whatever it is, whatever you are, tell me. I'm your wife now. I deserve to know."

She was right. Of course she was right. She'd always been right, from the very first day in the garden.

Garth took a deep breath, an unconscious gesture, and began to speak.

"What I'm about to tell you will sound like madness," he said. "It will contradict everything you've been taught about the world and your place in it. You may hate me when I'm finished. You may never want to see me again. But I need you to listen, and I need you to understand that every word I'm about to say is the truth."

She didn't flinch. Didn't pull away. Just stood there, holding his hands, waiting.

"I am nine hundred and seventeen years old," he said. "I was born in Rome, in the time of the emperors. I served in the legions before I was taken, transformed into something that is no longer entirely human. I age extremely slowly. I don't die, except by violence. I drink blood once a month to survive, though I've never killed anyone who didn't deserve it. I cannot walk in daylight. The sun would destroy me. And I have loved you, Basina Courtois, from the moment I saw you kneeling in that garden, with dirt on your hands and dusk's glow in your eyes."

He paused, watching her face. Waiting for the horror. The rejection. The scream that would summon help and end everything.

It didn't come.

"I know," she said quietly.

"You... what?"

"I know." A small smile played at her lips. "Not the specifics. Not the centuries or the blood or the sunlight. But I knew you weren't...

ordinary. I've known for months. The only question was whether you'd trust me enough to tell me."

He stared at her. "And you're not afraid?"

"I'm terrified." Her voice was steady, but he could hear her heart racing now. The rapid beat that betrayed her calm exterior. "I'm terrified and confused and I have about a thousand questions. But I'm not afraid of you. I've never been afraid of you."

"There's more," he said. "There's a choice you need to make. A choice I should have given you months ago, before the wedding, before everything. But I was a coward. I was afraid you'd say no."

"What choice?"

He told her about the Birthing. About what it meant, what it cost, what it offered. About the death of her human life and the beginning of something else. Something endless and strange and irrevocable. About the Hierarchy and its laws, and the danger they would both face if they were discovered.

He told her everything. Held nothing back. Gave her the full weight of the truth and waited to see if she could bear it.

When he finished, the moon had moved across the sky and the candles had burned low. Basina stood in the dim light, her expression unreadable.

"If I say no," she said finally, "what happens?"

"I leave. Tonight. You never see me again. You go on with your life, marry someone else, grow old, die." His voice cracked. "I go on existing, knowing what I lost."

"And if I say yes?"

"You die tonight. And then you wake up as something new. Something that will live beside me for centuries, if we're careful. If we're lucky."

She was silent, thinking. He could hear her heartbeat, steady now, the fear replaced by something else. Resolve.

"What's it like?" she asked. "Being what you are?"

"Lonely," he said honestly. "Dangerous. Strange in ways I can't fully describe. But also..." He searched for the words. "There's beauty in it. In watching the world change around you. In having time to truly know someone, truly learn them, truly love them." He cupped her face in his hands. "I've existed for almost a thousand years, Basina. And I've never loved anyone the way I love you. I never want to stop loving you. That's what I'm offering. Forever."

She reached up and covered his hands with her own.

"Then I choose you," she said. "Whatever that means. Whatever it costs. I choose you."

"You're certain? There's no going back. Once it's done."

"I'm certain." She smiled, and it was like watching the sun rise. Except the sun would never welcome him the way she did. "I've been waiting my whole life for something I couldn't name. Now I know what it was. I was waiting for forever."

She kissed him then, soft and certain, and Garth Van Demir felt something he hadn't felt in nine centuries.

Hope.

12

REBIRTH

The bedroom was still save for the distant hum of the refrigerator and Mimi's soft breathing from somewhere in the hall. Brianna had closed the curtains against the night, lit candles instead of switching on the lamps. It seemed appropriate, somehow. What they were about to do belonged to candlelight, to shadow, to the ancient dark.

Daphne sat on the edge of the bed, her hands folded in her lap, watching Brianna pace.

"You don't have to do this."

Brianna stopped. Turned. The candlelight carved hollows beneath her cheekbones, made her look older than she was. Older than she appeared, at least. Nearly nine centuries of existence, compressed into the face of a woman who might have been forty.

"I know I don't have to." Daphne's voice was steady. Calm in a way that made Brianna's chest ache. "I want to."

"Wanting isn't enough. You need to understand."

"I understand." Daphne rose from the bed and crossed to where Brianna stood, taking both her hands in her own. Her skin was warm. So warm. The warmth of a living heart, of blood that flowed the way blood was meant to flow. "I've understood for seven years, Bri. Ever since that first morning when you told me what you were."

"I told you about the feeding. The strength. The years." Brianna shook her head. "I didn't tell you about the pain. About what it feels like to have your body die and remake itself. About the hunger that comes after. The need that never entirely goes away."

"Then tell me now."

Brianna looked at this woman. This stubborn, patient, impossible woman who had waited seven years for something Brianna had sworn never to give. Seven years of friendship. Seven years of careful distance. Seven years of watching Daphne grow older, one day at a time, while Brianna remained frozen in the shape she'd worn since 1152.

And now Elijah was here. Now everything was about to burn.

"It will hurt," Brianna said finally. "Not like anything you've ever experienced. Your body will die, Daphne. Your heart will stop beating. And then something else will begin. A fever that feels like fire in your veins, like every cell is being torn apart and rebuilt from the inside out. It takes days. Two, maybe three. And during that time, you won't know who you are. Won't know where you are. Won't know anything except the pain and the change and the hunger growing inside you."

Daphne didn't flinch. Didn't look away. "What else?"

"After. When you wake." Brianna's voice dropped. "You'll be different. Stronger. Faster. But the world will be different too. Colors will be sharper. Sounds will be louder. And the hunger..." She closed her eyes. "The hunger is always there. A hollow space behind your ribs that never quite fills. You'll learn to manage it. To feed without killing, without losing yourself. But it takes time. And control. And there will be moments, especially in the beginning, when you'll want things that terrify you."

"Blood."

"Yes."

Daphne was quiet for a long moment. Her thumbs traced slow circles across Brianna's knuckles, a gesture so tender it made Brianna want to weep.

"I've thought about this," Daphne said. "Not just tonight. Not just this week. I've been thinking about it for years, Bri. Imagining what it would be like. What I would become." She lifted their joined hands, pressed a kiss to Brianna's fingers. "Sometimes I imagined myself as a monster. Something dark and hungry, lurking in shadows, no longer the woman I used to be."

"Daphne—"

"But that's not what I see when I look at you." Her eyes met Brianna's, dark and certain. "I see someone who fights for justice. Who feeds on fish blood so she doesn't have to hurt anyone. Who spent a century burning herself in the sun just to walk in daylight. That's not a monster, Bri. That's the strongest person I've ever known."

"I'm not strong. I'm terrified."

"Of what?"

"Of losing you." The words came out ragged. "Of watching you go through this and not being able to help. Of." She stopped, unable to continue.

Daphne cupped her face in both hands, forcing Brianna to meet her gaze. "You won't lose me. I'm choosing this. I'm choosing you. Whatever comes next, the pain, the hunger, all of it, I choose it. Because I love you. Because I want forever with you. And because..." She smiled, just slightly. "Because seven years of waiting is long enough, don't you think?"

Brianna laughed. A wet, broken sound that was almost a sob. "You're impossible."

"I'm pragmatic. There's a difference." Daphne leaned in and kissed her, soft and sweet, tasting of the wine they'd shared earlier and something uniquely her. "Now. Are you going to keep trying to talk me out of this, or are we going to do this together?"

Brianna thought about Garth. About a cottage in Lyon, centuries ago, when she had been the one lying down and he had been the one terrified. About the promise she had made on a mountainside after he'd vanished. That she would never do this to another soul.

But Daphne was right. Seven years was long enough.

And if Elijah came for her tomorrow, if this was the last thing she ever did, at least she would know that Daphne had chosen. That she hadn't taken this from her the way so many things had been taken from Brianna.

"Together," she said.

Lyon, 1152

"It will hurt," Garth said.

They stood facing each other in the candlelit cottage, the moon hanging full and heavy outside the window. The wedding dress lay draped across a chair. Basina had changed into a simple linen shift, practical for what was to come. Garth had removed his doublet, rolled up his sleeves. The intimacy of the moment was almost unbearable.

"I know," she said. "You told me."

"Not just the Birthing itself. The days after. The transformation. Your body will die, Basina. Your heart will stop. And then something else will begin. Something that feels like fire in your veins, like every cell in your body is being remade." He reached out and touched her face, his fingers trembling slightly. "I've seen it before. Watched others go through it. It's not peaceful."

"I'm not looking for peaceful." She covered his hand with her own. "I'm looking for forever."

He wanted to argue. Wanted to give her more time, more chances to reconsider. But she was looking at him with those remarkable eyes.calm and certain and utterly unafraid, and he understood that further delay would be an insult to the choice she'd made.

"There's one more thing," he said. "After tonight, you'll need a new name. Basina Courtois will be dead. As far as the world knows. You can't carry that identity into what comes next."

"I've been thinking about that." A small smile played at her lips. "I want to take your name. Van Demir. But I want a new first name, too. Something that marks the change."

"What did you have in mind?"

"Brianna." She said it slowly, testing the shape of it. "I've always loved that name. It means 'strong.' I think I'm going to need to be strong, aren't I?"

"Brianna Van Demir." He let the name settle into his mind, into his heart. "It suits you."

"Then that's who I'll be." She took a deep breath, squaring her shoulders like a soldier preparing for battle. "I'm ready."

But Garth wasn't. Not quite. There was one more thing he needed to say. One more truth he needed to give her before they crossed this threshold together.

"I love you," he said. The words felt inadequate, too small to contain everything he felt. "I've lived for almost a thousand years, and I've never said that to anyone. I've never felt it for anyone. But I feel it for you. Whatever happens tonight, whatever comes after. I need you to know that. I love you, and I will love you for as long as I exist."

Her eyes glistened in the candlelight. "I know," she whispered. "I've known since the garden."

He kissed her then. Gently at first, then deeper, trying to pour everything he couldn't say into the press of his lips against hers. She responded in kind, her hands finding his shoulders, pulling him closer. For a long moment, they simply held each other, two people on the edge of something vast and irrevocable.

Then she pulled back, just far enough to meet his eyes.

"Now," she said. "Before I lose my nerve."

They moved to the bed.

Garth had prepared it earlier. Clean linens, extra blankets for the cold that would come after, a basin of water and cloths for cleaning up. The practical details of transformation. He hated that he knew them so well, hated that he'd seen this process enough times to anticipate its requirements.

But he'd never been on this side of it before. Never been the one doing the Birthing. Never cared about the outcome the way he cared about this one.

Basina lay back against the pillows, her dark hair spreading across the white linen like ink on snow. She was so young. Eighteen years old, barely begun. And he was about to end her life so that she could begin again.

You could still stop, whispered a voice in his mind. Walk away. Let her grow old, let her die naturally, let her be human.

But she had chosen. She had looked at the truth of what he was, the full weight of what he was offering, and she had chosen him. To deny her that choice would be the greater cruelty.

He lay down beside her, propping himself on one elbow so he could see her face.

"I'm going to drink from you," he said quietly. "Not much—just enough to weaken you, to bring you to the edge. And then I'll give you my blood in return. That's what triggers the change. The exchange."

She nodded, her jaw set with determination.

"It's going to feel strange. Frightening, maybe. But I need you to trust me. I need you to know that I would never hurt you. Never."

"I trust you." No hesitation. No doubt.

He leaned down and pressed his lips to her throat, feeling her pulse flutter against his mouth. So alive. So fragile. So utterly, impossibly brave.

"I love you," he whispered against her skin.

Then he bit down.

She gasped. A sharp, startled sound that made his heart clench. But she didn't pull away. Didn't fight. Her hands came up to grip his shoulders, steadying herself as the first rush of her blood flowed into his mouth.

It was intimate in a way that nothing else could be. Not just the physical closeness, but the sharing. Her life force mingling with his, her essence becoming part of him. He could taste her courage in the blood. Her determination. Her love.

He drank carefully, counting the seconds, monitoring her heartbeat as it began to slow. Too little and the transformation wouldn't take. Too much and she would die before his blood could save her.

The line between success and failure was razor-thin.

Her grip on his shoulders weakened. Her breathing grew shallow. When he finally pulled back, her skin had gone pale, her eyes unfocused and distant.

"Basina." He cradled her face in his hands. "Stay with me. Just a little longer."

She tried to respond, but only a whisper emerged. Her heart was stuttering now, struggling against the blood loss, failing.

This was the moment. The threshold. If he waited too long, she would slip away entirely.

Garth raised his wrist to his mouth and bit down, opening a wound in his own flesh. Dark blood welled up. Thicker than human blood, richer, carrying the essence of nine centuries of existence.

He pressed the wound to her lips.

"Drink," he said. "Please. Drink."

For a terrible moment, nothing happened. She lay limp in his arms, her heartbeat fading to nothing, her chest still. He had killed her. He had taken too much, waited too long, and now she was gone, and he would have to live with that knowledge for the rest of eternity.

Then her lips moved.

Weakly at first, almost imperceptibly. But then stronger, more urgent. Her mouth closed around his wrist, and she drank. Her hands came up to grip his arm, pulling him closer, taking what he offered with a desperate, instinctive hunger.

He let her drink until the wound began to close, then gently pulled away. She made a sound of protest, a small wordless cry, but he shushed her, smoothing her hair back from her face.

"Enough," he said. "Now we wait."

The transformation took three days.

For the first hours, she simply lay still. So still that Garth had to press his ear to her chest repeatedly, listening for the heartbeat that had resumed after the exchange. It was there, faint but steady, working to spread the change through her body.

Then the fever came.

She burned. Not with illness, but with metamorphosis. Her human cells dying and being replaced by something new, something stronger, something that would last for centuries. She thrashed against the sheets, crying out in languages she didn't know, her body arching with pain that no medicine could ease.

Garth stayed beside her through all of it. He bathed her forehead with cool water. He held her hand when the convulsions grew violent. He whispered her name, her new name Brianna, over and over, an anchor to keep her from drifting too far into the darkness.

On the second night, she opened her eyes and didn't recognize him.

"Who are you?" Her voice was hoarse, raw from screaming. "Where am I? What's happening to me?"

"It's Garth. Your husband. You're safe. The change is almost complete."

She stared at him with eyes that were shifting, the brown of her irises slowly darkening toward something richer, deeper. Then recognition flickered across her face, and she began to cry.

"It hurts," she whispered. "Everything hurts."

"I know." He gathered her into his arms, holding her as gently as he could. "I know it hurts. But you're strong. You're the strongest person I've ever known. And when this is over, you'll never hurt like this again."

She sobbed against his chest until exhaustion pulled her back under.

On the third morning, she woke.

Garth had dozed off in the chair beside the bed, his hand still wrapped around hers. He came awake instantly when she stirred, his eyes finding her face in the gray pre-dawn light.

She was looking at him. Really looking, with eyes that were clear and bright and new. The deep brown transformed into something closer to amber, catching the light in ways that human eyes never could.

"Garth?" Her voice was different too. Stronger. More resonant.

"I'm here." He moved to sit on the edge of the bed, cupping her face in his hands. "How do you feel?"

She considered the question with the careful deliberation he'd come to love.

"Different," she said finally. "Everything is... more. I can hear your heartbeat. I can smell the candles that burned two nights ago. I can see the grain of the wood in the ceiling beam, every individual line." She looked at her hands, turning them over as if seeing them for the first time. "Is this what it's like for you? All the time?"

"You'll learn to filter it. To focus on what matters and let the rest fade into background noise. It takes practice, but it becomes natural eventually."

"And the hunger?" Her hand moved to her throat, a flicker of something dark passing across her features. "I can feel it. Like an emptiness behind my ribs. Is that...?"

"That's the blood hunger. It's strongest in the early days. We'll need to feed you soon. Properly. I have supplies prepared."

She nodded slowly, processing. Then her eyes found his again, and despite everything. The pain, the transformation, the alien hunger coiling in her chest. She smiled.

"We did it," she said. "We're really doing this. Forever."

"Forever," he agreed, his voice thick with emotion. "Brianna Van Demir. My wife. My partner. For as long as we both shall live."

"Which is going to be a very long time."

"Yes." He leaned forward and kissed her forehead, her cheeks, her lips. "A very long time."

She pulled him down onto the bed beside her, wrapping her arms around him with strength she was still learning to control. For a while, they simply lay there together. Two creatures outside of time, bound by blood and choice and something that might have been called fate if either of them believed in such things.

"I'm scared," she admitted quietly. "Of what comes next. Of the Hierarchy you told me about. Of being hunted for what we've done."

"I'm scared too," he said. "But we'll face it together. Whatever comes, whatever dangers we have to navigate. We'll face them together. I promise you that."

She was quiet for a long moment. Then: "Garth?"

"Yes?"

"Thank you. For telling me the truth. For giving me the choice." She pressed her face against his chest. "Most people go through their whole lives never really choosing anything. They just... follow the path that's laid out for them. But you gave me a real choice. You let me decide what my life would be."

He held her tighter, blinking back tears he hadn't felt in centuries.

"I couldn't have done it any other way," he said. "You deserved to know. You deserved to choose."

"And I chose you." She lifted her head to look at him, her new eyes bright with conviction. "Whatever happens next, remember that. I chose this. I chose you. And I would choose you again, a thousand times over."

Outside the window, the sky was lightening toward dawn. Soon they would need to close the shutters, retreat into darkness to wait out the day. Soon they would need to feed her, to begin the long process of teaching her how to live in a body that was no longer entirely human.

But for now, in this quiet moment between one life and the next, they simply held each other.

Basina Courtois was dead.

Brianna Van Demir had been born.

And whatever came next, they would face it together.

Whatever comes, Garth thought, you won't face it alone.

He believed it with all his heart.

He was wrong.

13

THROUGH TEARS

They made love that night. Real. Not temporary.

After seven years of careful distance, of touches that lingered a moment too long, of looks that said everything words couldn't. They finally stopped pretending. Daphne led her to the bedroom with a determination that brooked no argument, and Brianna followed because she was tired of fighting. Tired of holding back. Tired of being alone.

It was different this time. Different from the fumbling urgency of her youth, different from the comfortable intimacy she'd shared with Garth. This was something new: fierce and tender and achingly present. Daphne touched her like she was precious. Like she was real. Like she was worth the seven years of waiting.

Afterward, they lay tangled together in the darkness, Daphne's head resting on Brianna's chest, their breathing slowly returning to normal. The moonlight through the curtains painted silver stripes across the bed.

"I could stay here forever," Daphne murmured.

Brianna stroked her hair, memorizing the texture, the weight, the smell of her shampoo. Coconut and something floral. Such small details. Such precious, irreplaceable details.

"Daph," she said quietly. "I need to tell you something."

"Mm?"

"Tomorrow night. When I meet with Elijah." She felt Daphne tense against her but kept stroking her hair, kept her voice steady. "I don't think I'm coming back."

Daphne pushed herself up on one elbow, staring down at Brianna in the dim light. "What do you mean?"

"He's older than me. Stronger. More experienced in combat. And he has the backing of the Hierarchy. If I defy him openly, I'm not just fighting him. I'm fighting the entire power structure of my kind."

"Then don't defy him. Give him what he wants. Let him have Ross."

"I can't." Brianna reached up to touch Daphne's face. "Ross saved a boy's life. He's killing the ones who prey on humans. The monsters who give all of us a bad name. Handing him over to Elijah would be murder by proxy."

"And getting yourself killed would be better?"

"It would be right." The word felt strange in her mouth, unfamiliar after centuries of moral compromise. "I've spent lifetimes running. Hiding. Letting evil happen because confronting it was too dangerous. I can't do that anymore. Not with this."

Daphne was quiet. Her heartbeat was loud in the silence. Rapid, frightened, alive. So terribly, beautifully alive.

"There has to be another way," she said finally.

"Maybe. I'm going to try to find one. Ross has connections—people who fight the Baneful, who have weapons that can hurt Valensi. If I can get to him first, convince him to help me..." She shook her head. "It's a long shot. But it's the only shot I have."

"And if it doesn't work?"

"Then I'll face Elijah alone. And I'll probably die." She said it simply, without drama. A statement of fact. "But at least I'll die having done something that mattered. Something other than hiding."

Daphne sat up fully, the sheet pooling around her waist. In the moonlight, she looked like something from a Renaissance painting—dark skin luminous, eyes bright with unshed tears.

"No," she said.

"Daph—"

"No. I didn't wait seven years to lose you after one night." Her voice was shaking but resolute. "If you're going to face something that might kill you, then I'm going with you. I'm not letting you walk into that alone."

"You can't. You're human. Against Elijah, you'd be—"

"Then make me something else."

The words hung in the air between them. Brianna felt the world tilt, felt everything she'd built over eight centuries tremble on the edge of collapse.

"You don't know what you're asking."

"Yes, I do. You told me. The Birthing. The transformation. The blood." Daphne leaned forward, taking Brianna's hands in hers. "Make me like you. Make me strong enough to stand beside you."

"The change can take days. You'd be helpless until then. Worse than helpless. And even after, you'd be a fledgling. Weak. Hungry. Nothing that could help against someone like Elijah."

"Then at least I'd survive. At least I'd have forever to mourn you, instead of growing old alone wondering what might have been."

"That's not—" Brianna's voice broke. "Daph, I made a promise. After Garth. I swore. Never to take someone's humanity the way mine was taken."

"Your humanity wasn't taken. You chose it." Daphne squeezed her hands. "You told me the story. You stood in that cottage and you made a choice, fully informed, because you loved him and you wanted forever. That's what I'm asking for. The same choice. The same chance."

"It's not the same. He had centuries of experience. He knew what he was doing. I've never—"

"I don't care." Daphne's eyes were fierce now, burning with a conviction that left no room for argument. "I don't care if you've never done it before. I don't care if it's dangerous. I care about you. I've cared about you for seven years, and I will not stand by and let you die alone because of some promise you made to yourself eight hundred years ago."

"The promise was to protect people. To never—"

"The promise was to protect yourself." Daphne cut her off, not unkindly. "*You* told me that. It wasn't about preventing harm. It was about preventing loss. About making sure you never had to go through what you went through with Garth."

Brianna closed her eyes. The tears she'd been holding back finally spilled over, tracking hot lines down her cheeks.

"I can't lose you," she whispered. "Not like that. Not knowing I was the one who—"

"You won't lose me." Daphne released her hands and cupped her face instead, thumbs brushing away the tears. "I'm right here. I'm choosing this. I'm choosing you. And whatever happens tomorrow night, at least we'll face it together."

"Together." The word caught in her throat. "You keep saying that."

"Because I mean it. That's what love is, Bri. Showing up. Staying. Even when it's terrifying." She leaned forward and pressed her forehead against Brianna's. "I'm asking you to break that promise. For me. For us. Please."

Brianna opened her eyes. Daphne's face was inches from hers, beautiful and fierce and so full of life that it hurt to look at her.

She thought about Garth. About the garden, the courtship, the wedding night when he'd given her a choice that changed everything. He'd been terrified too. Terrified of losing her. Terrified of making the wrong decision.

But he'd trusted her enough to let her choose.

Could she do any less for Daphne?

"If I do this," she said slowly, "you need to understand what it means. Your human life ends tonight. Your family, your job, your identity. All of it. Gone. You'll have to start over. Build something new. And the first few years are... difficult. The hunger. The adjustment. Learning to control abilities you never knew you had."

"I understand."

"And there's no guarantee. The transformation is dangerous. I've never done it before. If I take too much, or not enough, or if something goes wrong—"

"I trust you." No hesitation. No doubt. Just like Basina, all those centuries ago. "I trust you with my life. With whatever comes after."

Brianna looked at her. Really looked, trying to memorize every detail of this moment. The moonlight on her skin. The love in her eyes. The stubborn set of her jaw.

"I love you," she said. "I've been afraid to say it. Afraid to feel it. But I love you, Daphne Jenkins. And I will love you for as long as I exist."

Daphne smiled through her own tears. "I know. I've always known."

She kissed her then, soft and certain, and Brianna tasted salt and surrender and the first stirrings of hope.

"Okay," she whispered against Daphne's lips. "Okay."

They prepared the bed together.

Clean sheets. Extra blankets for the cold that would come after. A basin of water and cloths on the nightstand. The small refrigerator key on a ribbon around Daphne's neck, in case. In case everything went wrong and Brianna wasn't there when she woke.

Don't think about that, Brianna told herself. *Don't think about anything except this moment.*

Daphne lay back against the pillows, her dark hair spreading across the white linen like ink on snow. She wore a simple cotton nightgown. Practical, comfortable. The kind of thing you'd wear to sleep, not to die.

But she was going to die tonight. Her heart would stop. Her lungs would cease. And then, if Brianna did everything right, something else would begin.

"Tell me again," Daphne said. "What it will feel like."

Brianna sat on the edge of the bed, her hand finding Daphne's. Their fingers intertwined. Mocha skin against pale, warmth against cool. Such a small thing. Such an enormous thing.

"First, I'm going to drink from you. Not much. Just enough to bring you to the edge. To weaken you enough that the change can take hold." She spoke carefully, clinically, the way Garth had spoken to her all those centuries ago. "It will feel strange. Like something vital draining away. But there's pleasure in it too. Our saliva releases endorphins. It won't hurt. Not this part."

"And then?"

"Then I'll give you my blood. That's what triggers the transformation. The exchange." Brianna squeezed her hand. "After that, the fever will begin. Hours of it. Maybe days. Your body will be remaking itself. Bones, muscles, blood. Everything dying and being reborn."

"Will I know you're there?"

"I don't know." Brianna's voice cracked. "I don't remember much of my own transformation. Just fragments. Pain. Voices. Garth's hand in mine." She looked down at their interlaced fingers. "I'll stay as long as I can. I'll be here when you wake."

She didn't know if that last part was true. Elijah was waiting. Ross was in danger. And the clock was ticking toward something terrible.

But she couldn't think about that now. Couldn't think about anything except Daphne's face in the candlelight, her eyes steady and unafraid.

"I trust you," Daphne said. "I trust you with my life. With whatever comes after."

"I love you." Brianna bent down and kissed her. Soft at first, then deeper, trying to pour everything she couldn't say into the press of her lips. "I've been afraid to say it. Afraid to feel it. But I love you, Daphne Jenkins. And I will love you for as long as I exist."

Daphne smiled through her tears. "I know. I've always known."

She kissed her again. And then, because there was nothing left to say, Brianna shifted her weight and pressed her lips to Daphne's throat.

She could feel the pulse there. Rapid but steady, brave and bright. The scent of her skin. The warmth of her blood, just beneath the surface.

Forgive me, Brianna thought. *Forgive me for what I'm about to do.*

Then she bit down.

Daphne gasped.

The pain was sharp. A bright, clean flash, there and gone in an instant. And then...

Something else. Something she hadn't expected.

Warmth flooded through her, radiating out from the place where Brianna's mouth met her throat. A strange, heavy pleasure that made her limbs feel loose and her thoughts go soft around the edges. She could feel Brianna drinking. Feel the slow, steady pull of blood leaving her body. But it didn't hurt. It felt like sinking into a warm bath. Like falling asleep after a long day. Like coming home.

This is what it feels like, she thought dreamily. *This is what she experiences when she feeds.*

Brianna's hands gripped her shoulders, steadying her. Daphne's own hands had risen without conscious thought, finding Brianna's back, pulling her closer. She couldn't tell anymore where she ended and Brianna began. They were connected now. Blood and flesh and something deeper, something that went beyond the physical.

The room began to fade at the edges. The candlelight grew dim. Daphne could feel her heartbeat slowing, could feel the darkness creeping in around the borders of her vision.

I'm dying, she realized. *This is what dying feels like.*

She wasn't afraid.

"Stay with me." Brianna's voice came from somewhere far away. "Just a little longer."

Daphne tried to respond, but her lips wouldn't move. Her body felt distant now, like something she'd borrowed and was returning. The last thing she saw was Brianna's face above her. Pale and tear-streaked, beautiful in the candlelight. And then the darkness swallowed her whole.

Brianna pulled back, her mouth slick with blood, her heart hammering in her chest.

Daphne lay motionless. Her eyes were closed. Her breathing had stopped. Her pulse, when Brianna pressed trembling fingers to her throat, was barely there. A thread. A whisper.

Too much. I took too much. She's dying, she's—

She bit into her own wrist, hard enough to open a wound. Dark blood welled up. Thick, ancient, carrying eight centuries of existence in every drop.

She pressed the wound to Daphne's lips.

"Drink," she whispered. "Please. Drink."

Nothing.

Daphne's lips didn't move. Her body didn't respond. She lay there, pale and still, looking for all the world like a corpse.

No. No, no, no—

"Drink, damn you." Brianna's voice broke. "I didn't come this far to lose you. I didn't break every promise I ever made to watch you die in my bed. DRINK."

For one terrible, endless moment, nothing happened.

Then Daphne's lips moved.

Weakly at first. A flutter, a twitch. Then stronger. Her mouth closed around the wound, and she *pulled*, and Brianna felt her blood flowing out of her and into this woman she loved more than she'd ever intended to love anyone.

Daphne's hands came up, gripping Brianna's arm with desperate strength. Her eyes were still closed, but her throat was working, swallowing, taking what was offered with an instinct that went deeper than thought.

There you are, Brianna thought. *There you are, my love. Come back to me.*

She let Daphne drink until the wound began to close, then gently—so gently—pulled her arm away.

Daphne made a sound of protest. Her hands reached for something that was no longer there. But she didn't wake. She was already sliding somewhere deeper than sleep, darker than unconsciousness.

The transformation had begun.

For the first hour, Daphne simply lay still.

Brianna sat beside her, holding her hand, watching her chest for signs of breathing. There were none. Not yet. The body was dead now, technically. The heart had stopped. The lungs were empty. But the change had begun beneath the surface. Something vast and slow and irrevocable.

Around the third hour, the tremors began.

Small at first. A twitch in Daphne's fingers, a flutter in her eyelids. Then larger. Her whole body began to shake, a fine vibration that built and built until she was convulsing against the sheets.

Brianna held her through it, pinning her shoulders down so she wouldn't hurt herself, murmuring words she wasn't sure Daphne could hear. "I'm here. I'm right here. It's going to be all right."

The fever came with the convulsions.

Daphne's skin went from warm to hot to burning. Sweat broke out across her forehead, soaking through the cotton nightgown, plastering her hair to her skull. Her breath came back in ragged gasps. Shallow, irregular, the lungs remembering how to work even as they were being remade.

Brianna bathed her face with cool water from the basin. Changed the sheets when they became soaked through. Talked to her constantly, even when Daphne gave no sign of hearing.

"I remember this," Brianna said, during a brief lull in the convulsions. "Garth stayed with me the whole time. Three days, he said later. Three days of fever and pain and not knowing who I was. But he never left. He held my hand through all of it."

She squeezed Daphne's fingers, felt the burning heat of her skin.

"I'm going to do the same for you. Whatever happens. I'm not going anywhere."

It was a lie. She knew it was a lie even as she said it. But she needed to believe it, just for a little while longer.

Somewhere around hour six, Daphne started to dream.

Or perhaps dream wasn't the right word. The visions came in fragments. Sharp and vivid and disconnected, like a film that had been cut into pieces and reassembled in random order.

She was walking across a stage.

Graduation. The robes were too hot, the cap kept slipping, but her mother was in the audience somewhere, and her advisor had just called her name, and she was walking toward a man in a suit who held a piece of paper that said she was a teacher now. That all those years of study had finally led somewhere.

Daphne Jenkins. Master of Education.

The crowd applauded. Her mother stood up, crying, waving a disposable camera like it was a flag. And Daphne felt—for one perfect moment—like she had finally become the person she was supposed to be.

Then the stage dissolved.

She was in the library now. UNCC campus, second floor, the section devoted to medieval literature. The air smelled of old paper and dust and something sweet—coffee, maybe, from the cafÃ© downstairs.

She was reaching for a book. *French Poetry of the Troubadours.* Her fingers closed around the spine just as another hand reached for the same volume.

She looked up.

Brown eyes. No—not brown. Darker. Deeper. The color of coffee left to cool too long, or rich earth after rain. Eyes that held centuries in their depths, though Daphne wouldn't understand that until later.

"Oh," the other woman said. "I'm sorry. Were you—?"

"No, please. You take it."

"We could share." A smile, hesitant but genuine. "I'm not in a hurry."

Brianna. The name wouldn't come until later, over coffee, after three hours of conversation that had felt like minutes. But Daphne felt it anyway—felt something click into place deep inside her chest, like a key turning in a lock she hadn't known was there.

This was important. This was the beginning of something.

The library dissolved.

She was in a bedroom now. Not Brianna's—her own apartment, before she'd started staying over more nights than not. The sheets were tangled. Moonlight fell through the window, painting everything in shades of silver and shadow.

Brianna lay beside her, tracing patterns on her bare shoulder, her touch feather-light.

"We shouldn't have done that," Brianna said quietly.

"Probably not."

"I told myself I wouldn't. Wouldn't let anyone this close again."

"And yet here you are."

A long pause. When Brianna spoke again, her voice was different—smaller, somehow. Younger. "I should go. Before this becomes something I can't walk away from."

Daphne turned to face her. Reached out and touched her cheek, feeling the coolness of her skin, the way she went perfectly still at the contact.

"What if I don't want you to walk away?"

"Daphne..."

"What if I want this to become something? What if I've been waiting for something to become for my entire life, and you're it?"

Brianna closed her eyes. A tear slipped down her cheek—Daphne caught it with her thumb, wondering at the salt and the cold and the weight of however many years lived behind those dark eyes.

"I'll hurt you," Brianna whispered. "I always hurt the people I love."

"Then hurt me. I'd rather be hurt by you than untouched by anyone else."

The memory dissolved.

And then—

She was somewhere else. Somewhere dark.

She was standing in front of a mirror, but the reflection wasn't hers. It was *something else*—something with her face, her body, but wrong. Its eyes were too dark. Its teeth were too long. When it smiled, it was the smile of a predator who has cornered its prey.

Monster, the reflection said. *That's what you're becoming. That's what she's turning you into.*

No. That's not—

Yes. Look at yourself. Look at what you're choosing.

The reflection leaned forward, pressing its hands against the glass from the inside. Its fingers were tipped with claws. Its mouth was stained with something dark and wet.

You'll want to hurt people. You'll crave it. The hunger never stops, Daphne. Never. It just gets quieter for a while, and then something triggers it, and all you can think about is the taste of blood on your tongue.

I won't. I won't let myself become—

You won't have a choice. The reflection laughed—a sound like breaking glass. *That's the beautiful thing about monsters. They don't choose what they are. They just ARE.*

The mirror cracked.

And Daphne fell screaming into the dark.

On the second night, Brianna almost broke.

She was exhausted. Drained in ways that went beyond the physical. The transformation was reaching its peak now—Daphne's convulsions had become almost continuous, her screams hoarse and broken, her body arching against the restraints Brianna had been forced to add with terrifying strength.

And Elijah was out there. Waiting. Planning.

Brianna could feel the clock ticking. Every hour she stayed here was an hour she wasn't dealing with the threat. An hour Ross sat in danger. An hour the Protector grew more confident that his prey was cornered.

But she couldn't leave. How could she leave? Daphne was still in the grip of the transformation, still lost somewhere in the fever and the pain. If Brianna walked out now, if something went wrong,

You can't save her by sitting here.

The thought was cold. Practical. The part of her that had survived eight centuries by making hard choices when hard choices needed to be made.

If Elijah finds you, if he comes here, she dies anyway. You both die. And everything you've sacrificed means nothing.

She looked at Daphne's face. The woman she loved, lost somewhere in the agony of becoming something new. The woman who had waited seven years for this. Who had chosen this, freely, knowing—or thinking she knew—what it would cost.

She chose, Brianna told herself. *She chose this. She knew the risks.*

But had she? Had she really understood what it meant to be abandoned mid-transformation? To wake up alone, hungry, confused, with nothing but a note and a key to a refrigerator full of blood?

You have to go.

She didn't want to. Every instinct screamed at her to stay, to hold Daphne's hand through the final hours, to be there when she opened her new eyes and took her first breath in her new body.

But the world didn't care what she wanted.

The world was burning, and she was the only one who could put out the flames.

Brianna bent down and pressed a kiss to Daphne's forehead. The skin was burning hot, slick with sweat, but she lingered there anyway, trying to memorize the feel of her.

"I'm sorry," she whispered. "I'm so sorry to leave you like this."

Daphne didn't respond. She was somewhere else now—somewhere beyond words, beyond comfort, beyond anything Brianna could offer.

"I have to try to stop him. I have to try to make this right. But I want you to know—" Her voice broke. "I want you to know that leaving you is the hardest thing I've ever done. Harder than becoming Solari. Harder than losing Garth. Harder than anything."

She straightened. Wiped her eyes.

Write the note, she told herself. *Do what needs to be done.*

She crossed to the small desk in the corner. A beautiful antique, eighteenth-century French, one of the few things she'd kept from her Paris years. And sat down with a sheet of paper and a pen.

The pen hovered over the paper.

Brianna had written letters before. Thousands of them, probably, across eight centuries. Love letters. Legal documents. Farewells to identities she was abandoning. The written word had been her companion through countless lives.

But she had never written anything like this.

My love—

No. Too dramatic. She crumpled the paper and started again.

Daphne—

I'm sorry. I'm so sorry to leave you like this. But I have to try to stop him. I have to try to make this right.

She stared at the words. They looked inadequate. Cruel, even. The kind of thing you wrote when you were abandoning someone, not when you were leaving the love of your existence to face a monster.

But what else could she say? That she was terrified? That she didn't expect to survive? That walking out this door might be the last thing she ever did?

There's blood in the kitchen. In the small refrigerator behind the pantry door. When you wake, you'll be hungry. Drink it. It will help.

Practical. She could be practical. Daphne would need that when she woke. Instructions, not apologies.

The transformation takes two to three days. The pain will pass. I promise. And when it's over, you'll be stronger than you ever imagined.

She paused, the pen trembling in her hand. There were so many other things she wanted to say. About Elijah. About the war that was coming. About the terrible purpose that had taken root in her heart since the moment she'd learned about the Hierarchy's corruption.

She wanted to tell Daphne about Garth. About what it felt like to lose someone so completely that you spent eight centuries searching for answers. About how she couldn't—*couldn't*—let that happen again. Not to Daphne. Not to the woman she loved.

But there wasn't time. And Daphne deserved better than excuses.

If I don't come back, Mimi will stay with you. She knows what you'll need. Trust her.

Mimi. Sixty-three years of telepathic companionship, of shared silences and understood grief. The cat would keep Daphne safe— would explain what was happening, would guide her through the first terrible hours of her new existence. It wasn't enough. It would never be enough.

But it was all she could give.

I love you. I have always loved you. And I will love you for whatever comes next.

She signed it simply: *—B*

Then she set down the pen and sat there, listening to Daphne's ragged breathing, watching the candles flicker in the darkness.

She deserves you, whispered a voice in her head. *She deserves you staying.*

Brianna closed her eyes. Felt the tears sliding down her cheeks.

Yes. Daphne deserved that. Deserved better than a note and an absence. But the world didn't give you what you deserved. The world gave you choices, terrible impossible choices, and you made them as best you could and lived with the consequences.

She stood. Folded the note. Placed it on the pillow beside Daphne's head, along with the small key on its ribbon. The key to the refrigerator where the blood was stored.

Then she looked down at the woman she loved.

Daphne's face was slack now, the convulsions finally easing. Her skin was still too hot, her breathing still too shallow, but there was something different about her. A settledness. Like the worst of the storm had passed.

She's going to wake up soon, Brianna realized. *Maybe hours. Maybe less.*

She's going to wake up, and I won't be here.

The grief hit her like a physical blow. Centuries of loss, and somehow this felt worse than any of it. Worse than Garth's disappearance. Worse than London. Worse than the century of burning herself in the sun.

Because this was a choice. Her choice. And she was making it with full knowledge of what it would cost.

I love you, she thought, looking down at Daphne's face. *I love you more than I ever intended to love anyone. More than I ever thought I could love again.*

And I'm leaving you anyway.

Because the only thing worse than leaving would be watching you die because I stayed.

She bent down. Pressed her lips to Daphne's forehead one last time. Felt the fever-heat of her skin, the faint flutter of her new heartbeat.

"I'll come back," she whispered. "I don't know when. I don't know how. But I'll find you again. I promise."

It wasn't enough. It would never be enough.

But it was all she had.

Brianna Van Demir straightened her spine, wiped her eyes, and walked out of the bedroom without looking back.

Behind her, Daphne burned with the fire of transformation.

Alone.

14

GONE

Eight years.

Eight years of traveling together, building lives and abandoning them, staying one step ahead of anyone who might notice that the young couple never seemed to age. Eight years of learning what she was, what she could do, how to navigate a world that would destroy her if it discovered the truth. Eight years of love so complete that Brianna sometimes forgot she had ever been anyone else.

They had settled in a small cottage in the mountains that autumn—a remote place, far from the nearest village, where they could live without scrutiny for a few years before moving on. Garth had business to attend to in the lowlands, arrangements for their next relocation. They moved constantly, never staying anywhere long enough to raise questions.

"I'll be back tomorrow night," he said, pulling on his traveling cloak as the last light faded from the sky. "Two nights at most if the roads are bad."

Brianna watched him from the doorway, reluctant to let him go even for a moment. "Must you?"

"The contact won't wait. And we need the new papers before winter sets in." He crossed to her and leaned down to kiss her. Soft, unhurried, the kiss of a man who had forever to spare. "I'll be back before you know it."

"You always say that."

"And I'm always right." He smiled, and her heart clenched the way it always did when he smiled at her. Nine centuries old, and he still looked at her like she was the most remarkable thing he'd ever seen. "Don't wait up for dawn. Get some rest."

"I haven't been resting. I've been savoring."

"Is that what we're calling it?" He kissed her again, laughing against her lips. "I love you, Brianna Van Demir."

"I love you too. Now go, before I make you stay."

He went.

She listened to his footsteps on the path outside, heard the soft whinny of the horse as he mounted, tracked the sound of hoofbeats until they faded into the night.

Then she closed the door and returned to bed, pulling the quilts up to her chin, content in the certainty that he would return.

He didn't come back the next night.

She wasn't worried. Not at first. The roads in this region were unpredictable, and autumn storms could delay travel for nights on end. She lit a fire, made herself dinner, read the book she'd been savoring. Normal evening things. Domestic things.

He didn't come back the night after that either.

Or the night after that.

By the fourth night, the worry had calcified into something harder. Something that sat in her chest like a stone, making it difficult to breathe. She paced the cottage through the dark hours, unable to settle, unable to focus on anything except the door that remained stubbornly closed.

Something's wrong.

She knew it the way she knew her own heartbeat. Garth wouldn't leave her waiting like this. Wouldn't let her worry without sending word. In eight years of marriage, he had never once failed to return when he said he would.

On the fifth night, she went looking for him.

The village where he'd gone to meet his contact was two nights' ride from their cottage. One night to reach the waystation where they kept a lightproof room, another night to complete the journey. Brianna pushed her horse as hard as she dared, reaching the waystation just before dawn, pacing in the darkness of that sealed room until sunset freed her again.

She arrived at the village as the last merchants were closing their stalls for the evening.

No one had seen him.

She asked at the inn where he usually stayed. At the merchant houses where he conducted business. At the church, the blacksmith, the handful of shops that made up the village's modest commerce. Everyone remembered Garth Van Demir. He was memorable, with his easy charm and generous coin. But no one had seen him in weeks.

"Perhaps he went elsewhere," the innkeeper suggested, eyeing her with the particular wariness reserved for women traveling alone. "Changed his plans."

"He wouldn't. Not without telling me."

"Men do strange things sometimes. Even the best of them."

She wanted to scream at him. Wanted to grab him by his grimy collar and shake him until he understood that Garth wasn't *men*, wasn't *sometimes*, wasn't the kind of person who simply vanished without explanation.

But she couldn't. Couldn't draw attention to herself, couldn't reveal what she was, couldn't do anything that might make things worse.

So, she thanked him for his time and left, her hands shaking, her mind racing through possibilities she didn't want to consider.

She searched for months.

Every contact Garth had ever mentioned. Every city they'd lived in, every friend they'd made, every thread of connection that might lead her to him. She traveled through the darkest hours, sheltering in crypts and cellars and the lightproof rooms that their kind maintained along the major routes. Winter storms and spring floods slowed her but didn't stop her, driven by a desperation that bordered on madness.

Nothing.

It was as if he had simply ceased to exist. No body. No grave. No rumor of violence or accident or betrayal. Just... absence. A void where her husband had been.

She went to the Hierarchy.

It was a risk. They had been living outside the official structures, their marriage unauthorized, her Birthing illegal. But she was past caring about consequences. If they punished her, at least she would have answers. At least she would know.

The Hierarchy representative who received her was coldly polite. Yes, they were aware of Garth Van Demir. Yes, they knew of his... activities. No, they had no information about his current whereabouts. These things happened sometimes. Valensi disappeared. It was the nature of their existence.

"But where did he go?" she demanded. "Someone must know something."

"If we knew, we would tell you." The representative's smile didn't reach his eyes. "I'm sorry for your loss."

Your loss. As if Garth were already dead. As if the matter were closed.

She left the Hierarchy's halls with nothing but questions and the growing, terrible certainty that she would never find answers.

The years passed.

Ten years. Twenty. Fifty. A century.

She kept searching at first. Following every rumor, investigating every lead, refusing to accept that he could simply be gone. But the leads dried up. The rumors faded. And eventually, even her desperate hope began to wither.

He wasn't coming back.

She didn't know if he was dead or alive. Didn't know if he'd left by choice or been taken. Didn't know if he'd ever loved her at all, or if eight years of happiness had been nothing but an elaborate lie.

That was the worst part. Not the grief. Grief she could have survived. But the *not knowing.* The endless, agonizing uncertainty. The questions that circled in her mind during the long nights, year after year after year.

Did he leave me? Was I not enough?

Did someone take him? Is he suffering somewhere, waiting for me to find him?

Is he dead? Has he been dead all along, while I've been searching for a ghost?

She would never know. That was the truth she eventually had to accept. Whatever had happened to Garth Van Demir, she would never know.

She went to the mountains.

The same mountains where they'd had their cottage, though the cottage itself had long since crumbled to ruins. She climbed through the dark hours until the air grew thin and the cold cut through her like a blade, until she found a peak so high that the world below seemed like a dream.

And there, alone with the wind and the stars and the weight of two centuries of grief, she made her promises.

Three vows, spoken to no one but herself:

I will never Birth another Valensi. I will never create a bond that can be broken the way ours was broken. I will never do to anyone what was done to me.

I will never kill another person. I will not become the monster that this world expects me to be. I will not let grief turn me into something Garth would not recognize.

I will never let anyone get close enough to hurt me like this again. I will build walls so high that no one can climb them. I will survive, and I will endure, and I will never, ever love like this again.

The wind carried her words away into the darkness.

She stayed on that mountain for two years. Alone. Silent. Sheltering in caves when the sun rose, emerging each night to stand beneath the stars. Learning to live with the hollow space inside her where her heart had been.

When she finally came down, she was someone different. Someone harder. Someone who had learned that love was not a gift but a wound, and the only way to survive was to never let anyone close enough to inflict it again.

Basina Courtois had died on her wedding night, eight years into forever.

Now the woman who had been Brianna Van Demir died too. Not her body, but something deeper. Something essential.

What remained was a survivor. A ghost wearing human skin. A creature of the night who had learned that the darkness was safer than the light.

She walked down from the mountain and into the centuries that followed, carrying her grief like a stone in her chest.

And she never stopped wondering what had happened to the man who had promised her forever.

15

THE HUNTER

The Mecklenburg County Jail was not the worst place Ross had ever slept.

That honor went to the back seat of his Civic during the months after his discharge, when no one would hire a veteran with a limp and a look in his eyes that made HR managers nervous. Or maybe the storage closet at Madronite Industries, where he'd caught naps between rounds before he'd learned to sync his schedule with Rufus's.

Rufus.

Ross closed his eyes and pushed the name away, the way he'd been pushing it away for ten years. Some wounds didn't heal. You just learned to work around them.

He lay on the thin mattress and stared at the ceiling, counting the cracks in the concrete. Forty-seven. Forty-eight. The same number as yesterday, and the day before. Three days in this cell, waiting for a public defender who hadn't shown up, eating food that tasted like cardboard, wondering if anyone at Hawthorn knew where he was.

They should. Temper monitored police frequencies. But extraction took time, especially when the cover story was complicated.

And this cover story was very, very complicated.

John Sebastian Ross had been a soldier once.

He still dreamed about it sometimes. The weight of his kit on his shoulders. The smell of dust and diesel and something burning in the distance. The faces of his squad—Martinez with his terrible jokes,

Chen who never smiled but always had your back, Sergeant Wheeler who'd taught him that leadership meant eating last and sleeping least.

He'd been good at it. Three deployments, zero men lost under his direct command. He'd believed in what they were doing. Believed in it the way you had to believe, or the sand and the heat and the constant grinding fear would eat you alive.

Then his body had betrayed him.

The IED hadn't made a sound. That was the part Ross remembered most clearly—the silence before the world turned inside out. One moment he'd been walking point, scanning the road for disturbances. The next he was on his back, staring at a sky that had turned the color of rust, his ears filled with a ringing that wouldn't stop for three months.

His left side hadn't worked right since. Shrapnel had carved channels through muscle and nerve, left him with a leg that dragged when he was tired and a hand that trembled when he was stressed. The Army doctors had been optimistic at first—*full recovery expected, just need time*—but the time had stretched into months, and the months into a medical discharge.

Honorable. They'd made sure to say that. Honorable discharge. Like the word could fill the hole where his purpose used to be.

The VA hospital in Charlotte smelled like industrial cleaner and quiet desperation. Ross had sat in plastic chairs that squeaked against linoleum, watching other broken soldiers shuffle past—men missing pieces of themselves, men whose eyes had gone somewhere far away and never quite come back. The counselor had given him pamphlets about job training programs. The physical therapist had taught him exercises he'd do religiously for two years before admitting they weren't going to fix what was wrong.

He'd bounced between jobs after that. Warehouse work where his leg gave out after six hours on concrete. Delivery driving until a customer complained about "the scary-looking guy" who'd brought their package. Night stocking at a grocery store until the manager found him crying in the break room at 3 AM, unable to explain why the fluorescent lights felt like artillery fire.

Nothing stuck. Employers looked at his limp and saw liability. They looked at his eyes and saw something they didn't want to name.

He'd been living in his Civic for three weeks—showering at the Y, eating gas station food, pretending his life wasn't falling apart—when he saw the posting for Madronite Industries.

Security guard. Night shift. No experience required.

It wasn't glamorous. But it was a paycheck, and it came with a break room where he could sleep between rounds. The hiring manager—a man named Temper Sloane—hadn't flinched when he saw the discharge papers.

"You've seen things," Sloane had said, studying him with eyes that seemed to hold more than they should. "Things that don't fit into neat little boxes."

"Sir?"

"Never mind." He'd smiled. "You'll do fine here, Mr. Ross. Just fine. Come on. Time to meet your partner."

Ross had met a lot of dogs in his life.

He had never met anything like Rufus.

The English Mastiff stood behind an eight-foot fence, watching them approach with eyes that promised violence. When he barked, Ross felt it in his chest. A deep, barrel-chested sound that seemed to vibrate the air itself.

"Jesus Christ," Ross breathed.

"Ain't he something?" Sloane raised his voice over the noise. "Rufus! Silence." The dog huffed, quieted, and sat. His eyes never left

Ross. "Two hundred and seventy-five pounds of pure energy. He's a good boy, though. Mean as all hell, but good."

"You sure he won't just kill me?"

Sloane laughed. "He's a guard dog, Ross. You just have to know how to win him over." He handed Ross a plastic bag with three pieces of raw meat. "Venison. His favorite. Keep your eyes down, let him sniff your left hand, have the meat ready in your right. And whatever you do, don't say 'good boy.' He's been trained to distrust that phrase."

"What do I say instead?"

"'You rock.' It's a Matt thing. DiBondra loves this mutt."

The introduction went better than Ross expected. Rufus sniffed his hand, accepted the venison with surprising gentleness, and then—after Ross said the magic words—pressed his massive forehead against Ross's leg like a cat demanding attention.

"Welcome to the Madronite team," Sloane said.

Four months. That's how long Ross worked the night shift with Rufus.

Four months of twelve-hour shifts, walking the perimeter of the seventy-acre compound, checking doors and windows while the Mastiff padded alongside him like a shadow. Rufus had been standoffish at first. Watching Ross with those calculating eyes, maintaining distance, never quite trusting.

Ross hadn't pushed. He'd learned patience in the Army, and he recognized wariness when he saw it. So, he just talked. Sat near Rufus during breaks and talked about nothing. About the service, about his mother, about the dreams that wouldn't let him sleep. He didn't expect the dog to understand. He just needed to fill the silence.

One night, three weeks in, Rufus crossed the distance and laid his massive head in Ross's lap.

Ross had frozen, afraid to move, afraid to break whatever spell had fallen over them. Then he'd reached down and scratched behind Rufus's ears, and the dog had let out a sound that was almost a purr.

After that, they were partners.

It happened on a Tuesday night, three weeks before Christmas.

Ross was doing his rounds. The same route he walked every night. Rufus was somewhere near the lab building, probably chasing gophers. The dog had a thing about small animals invading his territory.

The first sign that something was wrong was the barking.

Not Rufus's normal bark. The deep, rumbling announcement of a squirrel sighting or a suspicious shadow. This was something else. Frantic. Furious. The sound of a dog who had found something that didn't belong.

Then silence.

Ross broke into a run.

He found Rufus by the glass doors of the lab building, lying on his side, utterly still. When Ross knelt beside him, he knew before he touched the thick neck. The Mastiff's head lolled at an angle that no living creature could achieve.

Broken. Cleanly, efficiently broken.

Ross's hand was on his pistol before he saw the shattered lock on the doors.

He should have waited for backup.

The 911 call went out, but Ross didn't wait. Couldn't wait. Whoever had killed Rufus was still inside, and the rage building in his chest wouldn't let him stand still.

He moved through the darkened lab building on muscle memory, years of military training taking over. Low. Quiet. Controlled. The anger helped. Sharpened his senses, steadied his hands. He'd deal with the grief later. Right now, there was only the mission.

He found them in the hallway outside the closed lab.

Two of them. A man and a woman, well-dressed, beautiful in a way that seemed wrong under the fluorescent emergency lights. They were trying to force the vault door. The heavy metal barrier that protected Madronite's proprietary secrets. When they heard Ross approach, they turned.

And smiled.

"Another one," the woman said. Her teeth were red. "How delightful."

They moved wrong. Too fast. Too fluid. Ross's first shot caught the man in the shoulder; he barely flinched. His second shot hit the woman in the chest; she laughed.

Then they were on him.

The fight was a blur of pain and fury. They were stronger than anything Ross had ever faced, faster than should have been possible. The woman's nails raked across his chest like knives. The man threw him into a wall hard enough to crack the drywall.

But Ross had been trained by the United States Army, and he was running on pure rage.

He fought dirty. Fought desperate. Used everything in reach—a fire extinguisher swung like a club, a broken chair leg driven into the man's eye, his own blood making the floor slick enough to throw off their footing. He grabbed the woman and dragged her toward the emergency exit, toward the gray light of dawn that was just beginning to creep over the horizon.

The sunrise saved him.

When the light touched them, they screamed. Horrible, inhuman sounds that would echo in Ross's nightmares for years. The woman tried to run, but Ross tackled her, held her down while she burned, watched her face blacken and crack and crumble to ash.

The man had made it to the shadows. Had escaped.

Ross knelt in the parking lot, covered in blood and ash, and watched the sun rise over Charlotte.

Rufus was dead.

And monsters were real.

Temper Sloane found him there an hour later.

He'd walked out of the building like nothing had happened, stepped over the pile of ash, and crouched down in front of Ross with unsettling calm.

"You survived," he said. "Impressive."

"What—" Ross's voice was raw. "What were they?"

"Come inside. There's someone you need to meet."

He'd taken Ross to a part of the building he'd never seen—a sub-basement filled with equipment he didn't recognize. He'd cleaned Ross's wounds, given him water, waited while the shock faded into something harder.

Then he'd taken him to Matthew DiBondra.

DiBondra looked like someone's grandfather.

Silver-haired, almost 60 maybe, with steady hands. But his eyes.his eyes held the same weight Ross had seen in veterans who'd survived things they couldn't talk about.

"Mr. Ross," he said. "Please. Sit."

"What killed my dog?" Ross didn't sit. "What were those things?"

There was a quick, hardened expression that clouded DiBondra's face. "First off... MY dog. Second. They're called Valensi." DiBondra's voice was clinical. "They've existed for thousands of years. Most of them live quietly. Feed without killing, avoid detection. But some don't. Some hunt."

"Hunt."

"Humans. For sport, for pleasure, for reasons even they don't understand." DiBondra paused. "The two who broke in were looking for something in our closed lab. They found Rufus instead."

Ross thought about the woman's red teeth. The man's inhuman speed. The way they'd laughed when bullets hit them.

"Madronite," he said slowly. "It's not just furniture, is it?"

"No." DiBondra almost smiled. "The material we manufacture—it has properties. When formed into weapons, it can kill them. Permanently. It's the only thing that works, aside from sunlight."

"You make weapons to kill monsters."

"We make weapons. We train people to use them. We hunt the Valensi who've gone wrong. The ones who prey on humans." DiBondra leaned forward. "You fought two of them tonight, Mr. Ross. Untrained. Unarmed. Even killed one of them. Running on nothing but rage and military instinct. That's... remarkable."

"Rufus was my partner."

"I know. And I'm sorry." Grief flickered in DiBondra's eyes. "I'm sorry for your loss. But you're still here, and that presents us with a choice."

Ross knew what was coming. Could feel the shape of it before DiBondra said the words.

"We have a division called Hawthorn Securities. We train hunters. We give them weapons that work." He met Ross's eyes. "We give them a chance to make sure what happened to Rufus doesn't happen to anyone else."

Ross thought about the massive head in his lap. The trust it had taken for Rufus to cross that distance. The silence where barking should have been.

"When do I start?"

Ten years.

Ten years of hunting. Ten years of tracking Baneful through cities across the country, armed with Madronite blades and the training Hawthorn could provide. Ten years of ending threats before they could claim more victims.

Ten years of carrying Rufus's death like a stone in his chest.

The woman in the alley had been Baneful. Hunting teenagers. Five kills, maybe more. Marcus Williams would have been number six.

Ross had stopped her. Done his job. And now he was sitting in a jail cell because the cops had arrived thirty seconds too early.

Funny how that works, he thought. Save someone's life, end up in prison.

The cell door buzzed.

Ross sat up. Past visiting hours. Past everything hours, really. No one should be coming.

But someone was.

A guard appeared, face carefully blank. "You've got a visitor. Lawyer."

"My public defender finally showed up?"

"Something like that." The guard stepped aside.

The woman behind him was perhaps forty, with pale skin and dark hair in a professional bun. Well-dressed. Expensive. And her eyes.

Her eyes were old. Far older than her face. The kind of old Ross had learned to recognize. Had spent ten years hunting.

Valensi.

"Mr. Ross," she said. Her voice was calm, controlled, with a hint of something European underneath. "My name is Brianna Van Demir. And I think we need to talk."

16

FIRST CONTACT

Ross didn't move from the bed.

He'd spent ten years learning to read Valensi. Their tells, their weaknesses, the small signs that distinguished the compliant from the Baneful. This one moved like old money and carried herself like someone who'd stopped being afraid of anything a long time ago. The age in her eyes suggested centuries, not decades.

Old. Powerful. And standing in his cell like she owned the place.

"You're not my lawyer," he said.

"No." She stepped inside, and the guard pulled the door shut behind her. The lock clicked with mechanical finality. "But I am here to help you."

"A Valensi here to help the Hunter." Ross let out a short laugh. "That's a new one."

Surprise flickered across her face, quickly followed by reassessment. "You know what I am."

"Lady, I've been killing your kind for ten years. I know exactly what you are."

"Then you know I could have let the system handle you." She didn't sit, didn't move closer, just stood near the door with her hands folded in front of her like a prosecutor about to deliver closing arguments. "Assault and battery. Witness testimony that you were talking about monsters. A pile of ash where a body should be. You're looking at years, Mr. Ross. Maybe decades, if the DA decides to push for attempted murder."

"I didn't touch that kid."

"I know. I spoke with Marcus Williams this morning." She paused, letting that sink in. "He told me what really happened. The woman hunting him. The fight. The way she turned to ash when you killed her."

Dread settled in Ross's chest. "You talked to Marcus."

"I needed to understand what I was dealing with." Her voice was calm, almost clinical. "A Hunter operating in Charlotte. Five confirmed kills in the past three months. The Hierarchy has taken notice."

"The Hierarchy." He sat up slowly, ignoring the protest of muscles still sore from the alley fight. "So that's what this is about. You're here to clean up a mess."

"I'm here because someone else is coming to clean up the mess, and if he finds you first, you won't survive the encounter."

The words hung in the air between them. Ross studied her face, looking for the lie, the angle, the trap. He'd dealt with Valensi who tried to talk their way out of dying. They always had an agenda.

"Who's coming?"

"His name is Elijah. He's a Protector. An enforcer for the Hierarchy. One of the oldest. One of the most dangerous." Fear flickered across her expression before she buried it. "He's been dispatched to eliminate the Hunter threat. That means you."

"And you're warning me out of the goodness of your heart."

"I'm warning you because Elijah is a monster, and I won't help him destroy someone who was protecting an innocent boy."

Ross was quiet for a long moment. He'd met a lot of liars in his life. Soldiers who couldn't admit they were scared, officers who sent men to die with smiles on their faces, Valensi who begged for mercy right before they went for his throat. This woman wasn't lying. Whatever else she was, she believed what she was saying.

"What's your angle?" he asked. "What do you get out of this?"

"Survival." The word came out flat, honest. "Elijah and I have... history. He's already contacted me, demanded my help in finding you. If I refuse outright, he'll kill me. If I help him, I become complicit in murdering an innocent man." She met his eyes. "I'm looking for a third option."

"What kind of history?"

"The kind I don't discuss with strangers."

Fair enough. Ross could recognize a wound when he saw one. He'd stopped poking at his own years ago.

"So, what's the play?" he asked. "You break me out of here, I help you fight this Protector, and we all live happily ever after?"

"Nothing that simple." She moved to the small bench bolted to the wall and sat, the first sign of fatigue she'd shown since entering the cell. "Elijah is old. Older than me by millennia. He's survived for this long by being smarter and more ruthless than everyone else. If we face him directly, we die."

"Then, what?"

"I don't know yet." The admission seemed to cost her something. "I'm still working on it. But the first step is getting you out of here before he tracks you down. A jail cell is a cage, Mr. Ross. Right now, you're trapped exactly where he'd want you."

Ross considered this. She wasn't wrong. He'd been thinking the same thing for three days. But trusting a Valensi went against every instinct he'd developed since Rufus died.

"Why should I believe anything you're telling me?"

"You shouldn't." She said it without hesitation. "I'm a Valensi. You're a Hunter. Under normal circumstances, we'd be trying to kill each other." She leaned forward slightly. "But these aren't normal circumstances. Elijah is a threat to both of us. And the enemy of my enemy is, at minimum, someone worth talking to."

"You know I've killed Valensi."

"Yes."

"Doesn't that bother you?"

"The ones you've killed were Baneful. Predators who hunt humans for sport." Her voice was cold now, edged with contempt.

"They're an embarrassment to our kind. A reminder of what we can become if we stop caring about anything beyond our own appetites." She paused. "I've been alive for eight hundred and seventy years, Mr. Ross. I've never taken a human life. I feed on salmon blood and pretend to be normal and spend my nights wondering if any of it means anything. The Baneful you hunt? They're not my people. They're just monsters wearing familiar faces."

Ross stared at her. In ten years of hunting, he'd never heard a Valensi talk like this. The compliant ones avoided him; the Baneful tried to kill him. None of them had ever sat in a jail cell and explained their moral philosophy.

"You're different," he said finally.

"I'm old." A ghost of a smile crossed her face. "Old enough to have developed opinions."

"Hawthorn has files on you. Brianna Van Demir. Assistant District Attorney. No kills on record. No indication of Baneful behavior." He watched her reaction carefully. "They flagged you as compliant years ago. Low priority."

"I'm flattered."

"But they also flagged you as a potential asset. Someone who might be useful if the right situation came along."

Now she looked genuinely surprised. "I wasn't aware Hawthorn kept those kinds of files."

"We keep files on everyone. Temper's thorough that way." Ross swung his legs off the bed and stood, testing his balance. The cell was small enough that they were only a few feet apart now. "So here's my question: is this the right situation?"

"What do you mean?"

"I mean, are you actually willing to work with Hawthorn? Not just with me. With the organization. With DiBondra. With people who've dedicated their lives to policing your kind."

She was quiet. He could see her thinking, weighing options, calculating risks. Whatever she was, she wasn't impulsive.

"If it means stopping Elijah," she said finally, "then yes. I'm willing to work with whoever can help me do that."

"Even if it means betraying your own kind?"

"Elijah isn't my kind." The words came out hard, sharp-edged. "He's a predator who wears sophistication like a costume. He's been watching me for centuries, toying with me, using me for his own entertainment. Whatever loyalty I might have owed the Hierarchy died a long time ago."

Ross recognized that tone. He'd heard it in his own voice, back when he'd knelt in a parking lot covered in ash and dog blood.

Rage. Old rage, carefully controlled, but rage nonetheless.

"Okay," he said. "I'm listening. What do you need from me?"

"Right now? I need you to trust me enough to let me get you out of here." She stood, smoothing her jacket with practiced precision. "I have contacts in the legal system. I can make this arrest go away. Misunderstanding, witness recantation, whatever story works best. But I need you to cooperate. No more talk about monsters. No more cryptic statements that make the police think you're insane."

"And after I'm out?"

"We meet with your people. DiBondra, Temper, whoever's running Hawthorn these days. We share information." She met his eyes. "And we figure out how to kill a Protector before he kills us."

Ross thought about Rufus. About Marcus Williams, who'd almost died in that alley. About all the victims he'd avenged over the past decade, and all the ones he hadn't been fast enough to save.

This woman was Valensi. His enemy by definition. But she was also offering him something he'd never had before. An ally inside the monster's world. Someone who understood the enemy from within.

It was probably a trap. It was almost certainly going to get him killed.

But so was sitting in this cell waiting for a Protector to find him.

"One condition," he said.

"Name it."

"You mentioned the boy. Marcus. He saw things he shouldn't have seen. Knows things that could get him killed."

"I've already taken care of it." Something softened in her expression. "I helped him... process the experience. He won't remember the details. Just enough to know he should be careful. Stay in the light."

"You can do that? Alter memories?"

"I can smooth edges. Soften trauma. It's not erasure. Just... gentle persuasion." She paused. "I don't do it often. And never without good reason."

Ross nodded slowly. It wasn't ideal. The idea of a Valensi messing with a kid's head made his skin crawl. But Marcus was alive, and safe, and wouldn't spend the rest of his life seeing monsters in every shadow.

"Okay," he said. "Get me out of here. And then we talk to Temper."

Brianna Van Demir allowed herself a small smile.

"I'll have you out by morning," she said. "Try to get some sleep, Mr. Ross. The next few days are going to be difficult."

She turned and knocked on the cell door. The guard appeared, blank-faced and obedient, and let her out without a word.

Ross stood in the silence she left behind, wondering what the hell he'd just agreed to.

Then he lay back down on the thin mattress and stared at the ceiling.

Forty-seven cracks. Forty-eight.

Tomorrow, everything changed.

17

THE MEETING

True to her word, Brianna had Ross out by morning.

The paperwork was impressive—witness recantation, prosecutorial discretion, a judge who signed the release order without asking questions. Whatever strings she'd pulled, they were the kind that didn't leave fingerprints. By 9 AM, Ross was standing in the parking lot of the Mecklenburg County Jail, blinking in the sunlight like a man emerging from a cave.

Brianna was waiting in a black sedan, engine running.

"Get in," she said through the open window. "We have a meeting."

Ross climbed into the passenger seat and studied her in the morning light. She looked different from the night before—less composed, more human. There were shadows under her eyes that hadn't been there in the dim cell. She'd been up all night, he realized. Pulling strings. Making calls. Doing whatever Valensi did when they needed to manipulate the human world.

"Where are we going?"

"Madronite Industries." She pulled out of the parking lot and headed north. "Temper's expecting us."

"You called him?"

"He called me. Apparently, you reached out last night." She glanced at him. "He seemed... intrigued."

Ross had used his one phone call to contact Hawthorn's emergency line. He'd given them the basics—a Valensi who wanted to help, a Protector incoming, a situation that didn't fit any of the standard protocols. Temper had listened without interrupting, then said four words: "Bring her to me."

"Temper doesn't get intrigued easily," Ross said. "You made an impression."

"I've had a lot of time to practice making impressions."

They drove in silence for a while. Charlotte slid past the windows—office buildings and strip malls and the ordinary infrastructure of a city that had no idea what lurked in its shadows. Ross watched the familiar streets and thought about Rufus, about the night everything changed, about the decade he'd spent hunting monsters in these same neighborhoods.

Now he was riding shotgun with one of them.

"You're thinking about whether you made the right choice," Brianna said. It wasn't a question.

"I'm thinking about a lot of things."

"For what it's worth, I'm asking myself the same question." She turned onto North Graham, heading toward the Tryon Hills area. "Trusting a Hunter goes against every instinct I've developed over the centuries. But instinct isn't the same as wisdom, and right now, wisdom says we need each other."

"Pretty speech."

"I've had time to practice those too."

Madronite Industries sprawled across seventy acres of fenced land, looking exactly like what it pretended to be—a successful manufacturing company with nothing to hide. Ross knew better. He'd walked every inch of this compound in the dark, back when his only partner was a 275-pound Mastiff who'd trusted him with his life.

The guard at the gate waved them through without checking IDs. They parked near the main building, and Brianna killed the engine.

"Before we go in," she said, "there are things you should know about me. Things Temper will probably tell you anyway, but you should hear them from me first."

"I'm listening."

"I was born in 1152. Lyon, France. I was human until I was eighteen, when my husband—" She paused, and Ross saw something flicker across her face. Pain, carefully controlled. "When the man I loved gave me a choice. Humanity or eternity. I chose eternity."

"That's in the file."

"The file doesn't have everything." She gripped the steering wheel, staring straight ahead. "It doesn't know that I've spent the last eight centuries hiding from the Hierarchy. That I've broken their laws just by existing—my Birthing was never authorized. It doesn't know about London, or what Elijah did to me there, or why I became Solari."

"Solari?"

"Valensi who can walk in daylight. It takes decades of... conditioning. Burning yourself in the sun, over and over, until your body adapts." Her voice was flat, clinical. "I spent a century doing that. Because I needed to hide somewhere Elijah couldn't follow."

Ross processed this. A century of deliberate burning. The kind of pain that would break most people, most creatures, into pieces.

"Why are you telling me this?"

"Because if we're going to work together, you need to understand what's at stake for me. This isn't just about surviving a Protector. This is about everything I've built, everything I've protected, for nearly a millennium." She finally looked at him. "I'm trusting you with my life, Mr. Ross. I need to know that trust isn't misplaced."

He thought about Rufus again. About the night he'd knelt in ash and blood and decided that some things were worth dying for.

"It's not," he said.

She nodded once and opened her door. "Then let's go meet Temper."

Temper Sloane hadn't changed.

Same sharp eyes, same easy manner, same way of making you feel like he knew exactly what you were thinking and found it mildly amusing. He met them in the lobby and shook Ross's hand with genuine warmth.

"J.S. Good to see you in one piece. The boys were getting worried."

"The boys can worry less. I'm fine."

"You got arrested standing over a pile of ash talking about monsters. That's not fine—that's sloppy." But Temper was smiling as he said it. He turned to Brianna and studied her. "Ms. Van Demir. I've heard a lot about you."

"Likewise, Mr. Sloane."

"Temper. Everyone calls me Temper." He gestured toward the elevators. "Come on. We've got a lot to discuss, and I'd rather do it somewhere without windows."

The sub-basement was exactly as Ross remembered it—clean, clinical, filled with equipment that looked like it belonged in a science fiction movie. Temper led them to a conference room and closed the door behind them.

"Coffee? Water? Something stronger?"

"Information," Brianna said. "I'd like to know what I'm walking into."

Temper smiled. "Direct. I like that." He settled into a chair and gestured for them to sit. "What do you know about Hawthorn Securities?"

"You hunt Valensi. You have weapons that work. You operate outside any official structure, which means either you have very powerful patrons or very deep pockets." She paused. "Probably both."

"All true. But that's what we do—not why we do it." Temper leaned back. "The supernatural world is failing to police itself. Has been for centuries. The Hierarchy talks a good game about maintaining secrecy, about punishing those who break the rules, but in practice?" He shook his head. "They protect their own. The powerful ones, anyway. The ones with connections."

"Like Elijah."

"Like Elijah." Temper's expression hardened. "Matthew DiBondra founded this company because he watched a Valensi kill his father. He was eight years old. Vacation in the Aegean. Some ancient bloodsucker decided the family looked like dinner, and the Hierarchy did nothing. 'Regrettable incident. We'll look into it.' That's what they told his mother."

Ross watched Brianna's face. She didn't flinch, but recognition shifted in her eyes. Understanding.

"He spent his life building this," Temper continued. "The material, the weapons, the organization. Not for revenge—Matthew's not the vengeful type. For regulation. Someone has to hold your kind accountable when the Hierarchy won't."

"And you decided I could be useful for that."

"We decided you were interesting." Temper pulled a folder from the table and slid it toward her. "Eight hundred seventy years old. No confirmed kills—human or Valensi. Feeding exclusively on animal blood for the past three centuries at least. Solari status, which puts you in a very exclusive club." He tapped the folder. "You've been on our radar for a long time, Ms. Van Demir. We just never had a reason to make contact."

"And now you do."

"Now we have a Protector coming to Charlotte. One of the oldest and most dangerous. And we have a Valensi who apparently hates him enough to risk everything by opposing him." Temper spread his hands. "That's not just interesting. That's an opportunity."

"An opportunity for what?"

"To send a message." Temper's voice was quiet now, serious. "The Hierarchy thinks they're untouchable. They think humans are cattle, to be managed and fed upon at will. They think Protectors are gods—invincible, eternal, beyond consequence." He leaned forward. "What happens when a Protector dies? When one of the oldest and most feared enforcers in the Hierarchy gets taken down by a Valensi and a Hunter working together?"

Brianna was silent. Ross could see her thinking, calculating, weighing the implications.

"It would change things," she said finally. "The balance of power. The assumptions everyone operates under."

"It would prove that no one is untouchable. That the Hierarchy's protection isn't absolute." Temper smiled—a thin, dangerous expression. "And it would make Hawthorn Securities the most valuable ally any Valensi could have. The ones who want to live quietly, who don't prey on humans, who just want to exist without being crushed by ancient politics? They'd know there's someone they can turn to."

"You want to build a coalition."

"I want to build a better world. One where creatures like you don't have to hide from creatures like Elijah." He stood. "But first, we need to survive the next forty-eight hours. Which brings us to the practical matter at hand."

He walked to a cabinet and pulled out a case, setting it on the table. Inside, nestled in foam padding, was a knife. The blade was strange—not quite metal, not quite wood, with a grain pattern that seemed to shift in the light.

"Madronite," Ross said.

"The real stuff. Not the furniture-grade composite we sell to the public." Temper lifted the knife carefully. "This is what we make in the closed lab. Weapons designed specifically to kill Valensi. One good hit and it spreads through the system—cellular disintegration, impossible to heal." He offered it to Brianna. "Consider it a gift."

She took it, turning it over in her hands. "You're arming a Valensi with a weapon designed to kill Valensi."

"I'm arming an ally with the tools she needs to survive." Temper returned to his seat. "Now. Tell me everything you know about Elijah. His patterns, his weaknesses, his obsessions. And then we'll figure out how to kill him."

Brianna set the knife on the table and began to talk.

18

THE PLAN

They talked for hours.

Brianna told them everything she knew about Elijah—his age, his methods, his position in the Hierarchy. She told them about his obsession with control, his telepathic abilities, the way he collected people the way other creatures collected art. She told them about London, in broad strokes, enough to convey the danger without reliving the details.

She did not tell them about Garth. Some wounds were too deep to share with strangers.

Temper listened with the focused intensity of a man cataloging weapons. Ross sat silently, processing, occasionally asking questions that revealed more tactical knowledge than Brianna had expected. They were both professionals, she realized. Different sides of the same war.

"His telepathy," Temper said. "How strong?"

"Stronger than anyone I've ever encountered. He can override motor control—make you sit, stand, walk toward him, even if you're fighting it with everything you have." She remembered the townhouse, the paralysis, the way her body had betrayed her. "I don't know if there's a range limit. I've never been far enough away to test it."

"Can you resist?"

"Partially. My age gives me some protection—older Valensi are harder to control. But against Elijah?" She shook her head. "I could slow him down. I couldn't stop him."

"What about Ross?"

"Humans are harder to affect. There are other mental capabilities that work rather well on humans. The telepathy works best on

Valensi—something about neural compatibility. He might be able to push through where I couldn't."

Ross shifted in his chair. "Might isn't the same as will."

"No. But it's better than nothing."

Temper stood and walked to a whiteboard mounted on the wall, picking up a marker. "Let's map this out. Elijah arrives in Charlotte to eliminate a Hunter threat. He contacts you, demands your help. You refuse. What happens next?"

"He comes for me." Brianna's voice was flat. "Either to force my compliance or to punish my defiance. Probably both."

"Where? When?"

"He'll want privacy. Somewhere he can take his time." She thought about his patterns, the things she'd pieced together over two centuries of watching for his shadow. "He prefers symbolic locations. Places that mean something to his target."

"Meaning?"

"Meaning he knows about Daphne. Knows where she works, where she lives, what she means to me." The words tasted like ash. "He'll choose somewhere that makes his threat clear."

Temper wrote on the board: Location - symbolic. Target's vulnerability.

"What about timing?"

"He's not Solari. He can only move at night." Brianna paused, thinking. "He'll want to feed first—he always does before a significant encounter. Gives him strength, clarity. So late night, probably. 3 or 4 AM. After he's hunted, before dawn forces him to ground."

Timing: 3-4 AM. Post-feeding.

"Weapons," Ross said. "You said bullets don't work. What does?"

"Sunlight. Madronite, apparently." She gestured at the knife on the table. "Fire, if it's hot enough and sustained long enough. Decapitation, if you can get close enough to manage it."

"What about that sword you mentioned? The one from your trainer?"

Brianna felt a flicker of surprise. She'd mentioned Asaro's gift in passing, hours ago, a detail she hadn't expected him to retain. "It's Japanese. Old. Gifted to me about two hundred years ago by a Valensi who trained me in combat."

"Where is it?"

"My house. Hidden."

"Can it kill Elijah?"

"It can hurt him. Whether it can kill him..." She shrugged. "He's old. Very old. The older we get, the harder we are to destroy. But a blade through the heart will slow anyone down."

Temper wrote: Assets: Madronite knife. Japanese sword. Sunlight (if timed right).

"Here's what I'm thinking," he said, capping the marker. "We don't wait for him to come to us. We choose the ground. We set the terms."

"How?"

"You said he wants symbolic locations. So, we give him one." Temper turned to face them. "Evergreen Cemetery. It sits right across from Eastway Middle School."

Brianna felt her chest tighten. "Daphne's school."

"Exactly. He'll see the connection. He'll appreciate the poetry of it." Temper's voice was cold, practical. "We position you there before he arrives. Let him find you on ground we've prepared. Ross takes high position with a clear line of sight. I'll have a team on standby—not to engage, but to contain. Make sure he can't run."

"And then?"

"And then you fight him. You keep him busy until sunrise, if you can. If not..." He nodded toward the knife. "You use what we've given you."

Ross leaned forward. "What about me? I just watch?"

"You wait for an opening. Elijah won't consider you a threat—you're human, wounded, nothing but prey in his eyes." Temper smiled grimly. "That's his mistake. When he's focused on Brianna, you move. One good hit with Madronite, and it's over."

The room fell silent. Brianna stared at the whiteboard, at the neat lines and bullet points that reduced her survival to strategy and tactics. It was a good plan. Temper knew what he was doing.

But plans had a way of falling apart when ancient monsters got involved.

"There's something else," she said quietly.

Both men looked at her.

"Daphne." The name caught in her throat. "She's... I Birthed her. Last night. She's at my house, transforming. Alone."

Ross's expression didn't change, but understanding flickered in his eyes. Temper was harder to read.

"You Birthed someone," Temper said slowly. "Last night. And then you came here."

"I didn't have a choice. Elijah was coming, and she demanded—" Brianna stopped, took a breath. "She wanted to be strong enough to help. To stand beside me. I couldn't refuse her. Not after everything."

"How long does the transformation take?"

"As long as three days. Depends on the person. She'll wake up hungry, disoriented, alone." Brianna's hands were clenched in her lap. "I left her blood. Instructions. But I won't be there when she wakes."

"Because you might be dead by then."

"Yes."

Temper was quiet. Then he nodded once. "We'll send someone to check on her. Discreetly. Make sure she has what she needs."

"She doesn't know anything about Hawthorn. About any of this."

"She will. Eventually." He held up a hand before she could protest. "Not now. Not until this is resolved. But if you survive, Ms. Van

Demir, we're going to need to have a longer conversation about alliances and obligations."

It wasn't a threat. It wasn't a promise. It was simply a statement of fact—the kind of pragmatic observation that Brianna had learned to expect from people who thought in terms of assets and liabilities.

"Understood," she said.

They spent another hour working through details.

Positions. Timing. Contingencies. What to do if Elijah brought backup, if he didn't take the bait, if everything went sideways. Ross asked questions that revealed the depth of his training—sight lines, retreat routes, communication protocols. Temper answered with the ease of someone who'd planned a hundred operations and survived most of them.

By the time they finished, the afternoon sun was slanting through the narrow basement windows.

"One more thing," Temper said as they stood to leave. "The sword. You said it's at your house?"

"Hidden in the living room. Under a floorboard by the fireplace."

"Ross should retrieve it. Before tonight."

Brianna hesitated. The sword was precious—not for its material value, but for what it represented. Asaro had given it to her as a symbol of trust, a recognition that she'd mastered the skills he'd taught her. Letting a Hunter into her home, into her secrets...

But Temper was right. If the plan worked, she'd need every weapon available. And if it didn't work, the sword's hiding place wouldn't matter anyway.

She pulled out her phone and typed a message to Ross: the address, the location of the hidden floor panel, the combination to the lockbox inside. Practical information, stripped of sentiment.

"Done," she said.

Ross checked his phone, nodded once. "I'll get it. Meet you at the cemetery?"

"4 AM. Eastern edge, near the oldest graves. That's where he'll come."

"How do you know?"

"Because that's where I'd come." She managed a thin smile. "We're not as different as we pretend to be. Elijah and me. We both appreciate the drama of a good setting."

Ross studied her for a moment—the kind of look that suggested he was reassessing something he'd thought he understood. Then he turned and left without another word.

Temper walked her to the elevator. At the door, he paused.

"You know this might not work."

"I know."

"You might die tonight."

"I've been dying for eight hundred years, Mr. Sloane." She stepped into the elevator. "At least this time it will be for something that matters."

The doors closed between them.

Brianna rode up alone, watching the floor numbers climb, thinking about Daphne burning in an empty house. About Ross retrieving a sword he didn't understand. About Elijah, somewhere in the city, preparing for a hunt he thought he'd already won.

4 AM, she thought. Evergreen Cemetery. One way or another, this ends tonight.

The elevator opened onto the lobby, and she walked out into the afternoon sun.

19

MEETING

The diner was the kind of place that asked no questions and remembered no faces. Vinyl booths, fluorescent lighting with one tube flickering, a laminated menu that hadn't changed since 2009. Ross was already in the back booth when Brianna arrived, a coffee cup in front of him that he wasn't drinking.

She slid into the seat across from him without preamble.

"You texted," she said.

"I wanted to talk. Not in the building." He turned the coffee cup a quarter rotation, a habit she was coming to recognize — not nervous, just needing the hands occupied. "Before tonight."

The server appeared. Brianna ordered coffee she didn't intend to drink, because it seemed necessary. When the server left, the silence between them held without being uncomfortable. Two people who'd both learned not to rush.

"Say what you came to say," she said finally.

Ross looked at his cup. "Temper's good at what he does. Making it feel like everybody wins. You get Elijah stopped. He gets a dead Protector and a living asset. We all go home satisfied."

"You think the framing is false."

"I think the goals don't fully overlap." He looked up. "You want to survive tonight. He wants you to survive so you can be useful later. Those aren't the same thing."

Brianna considered this. Outside, a truck rumbled past and rattled the window in its frame. "And you?"

"I already told you."

"Tell me again."

He set the cup down. "I want you to be alive at sunrise. That's it. Not the political outcome. Not the leverage on the Hierarchy. Just — sunrise, and you're breathing." A pause. "That's what I'm bringing to the table tonight. I thought you should know."

She looked at him for a moment — the careful, long-learned assessment she'd developed over centuries, the reading of whether someone's sincerity was genuine or performed. With most people it took seconds. With Ross, she found she didn't have to do it at all. He was one of the most transparent people she'd ever met, which she suspected he would find insulting.

"You think I don't know what I'm worth to Temper," she said.

"No. I think you know exactly what you're worth to him and you've decided it's acceptable."

"Because it is. He's the most capable ally available to me tonight. The reasons he has for wanting Elijah dead don't have to be mine. They only have to work."

Ross was quiet for a moment. Then: "How many times have you gone into something thinking that?"

"More than I'd like to say."

"How many times has it worked out the way you expected?"

She didn't answer immediately. The server came back with her coffee and went again without a word.

"Less than I'd like to say," she admitted.

Something shifted in his expression — not triumph, nothing like that. More like recognition. "You've already decided tonight might not go well."

"I've decided tonight is worth the cost."

"That's not the same thing."

"No. It isn't." She looked at him directly. "I'm eight hundred and seventy years old, Ross. I've outlived more people than I can name. I stopped being surprised when survival turned out to be a narrower concept than I'd planned." She paused. "That isn't despair. It's arithmetic."

"Arithmetic."

He repeated the word like he was wasn't certain of its meaning.

"I calculate what I have to spend and I spend it. If the calculation tonight says the fight costs more than I have—" She spread her hands. "Then it costs what it costs."

Ross looked at her for a long moment.

"You know what's interesting," he said slowly, "is that you make that sound like wisdom. Eight hundred years of narrowing down what you're willing to ask for until you're not asking for anything."

"That's not—"

"It's what it sounds like from here." He wasn't angry. His voice stayed flat, considered — the voice of someone choosing words with care. "I've met guys like that. Not cowards. The opposite. They go in lean, nothing attached, nothing to lose. Best soldiers in the room, right up until they decide they're already spent." He wrapped both hands around the mug. "I'm not going to stand on that hilltop watching your six while you run the arithmetic on what you're worth."

The fluorescent tube above the counter flickered. Outside, Charlotte moved through its evening.

"What would you prefer," Brianna said, "as an alternative?"

"You walk out of that cemetery." His tone hadn't changed. "Not because the numbers add up. Because you decide you're walking out, and then we find a way to make that happen."

"Those aren't always different things."

"They are in the moments that count." He picked up his cup and finally drank from it, a grimace suggesting it had gone cold. "Rufus was the best hunter I ever worked with. Read every scene faster than anyone. He went into that building because the numbers worked. Threat level, entry point, timing. Perfect math."

He set the cup down.

"Perfect math got him killed."

Brianna was quiet.

"I'm not interested in your perfect math," Ross said. "I'm interested in you coming out of that cemetery so we can figure out what comes next. That's why I'm going to be up there tonight." A pause. "Not Temper's agenda. Not the Hierarchy." Another. "You. Specifically."

She had not been spoken to that way in a very long time. Not the sentiment — she had Daphne, she had the ghost of Garth, she had known love in more forms than most people could count. But this specific thing: being named as a particular person worth protecting, for no reason of obligation or history or politics. Just: you. Specifically.

She did not know what to do with it, so she did what she always did.

"Don't make promises about things outside your control," she said.

"Fair enough." He didn't push it. "But I'm going to try. That's what I'm telling you."

She looked at him across the table. This damaged, precise, entirely transparent man who had spent ten years turning grief into purpose and was only now beginning to understand that purpose wasn't the same as meaning.

"All right," she said.

It was not a large thing. It meant less than either of them might have wished. But it was more than she had offered anyone in a long time, and they both knew it.

Ross left a ten on the table and stood.

"I'll get the sword. See you at the cemetery."

"Quarter to four."

"Quarter to," he agreed.

He walked out into the evening without looking back.

Brianna sat with the coffee cooling in her hands, listening to the traffic, thinking about arithmetic. About the specific, uncomfortable difference between spending what you had and deciding it was worth spending.

About what it cost, and who was counting.

20

THE FLEDGLING

The house was quiet when Ross arrived.

Too quiet. He'd been told to expect a woman in the middle of transformation—three days of fever and pain, unconscious and helpless. What he found instead was a Chartreux cat sitting on the porch railing, watching him with eyes that held far too much intelligence.

"You're the Hunter."

The voice came from nowhere. Ross's hand went to his knife before he realized the cat's mouth hadn't moved.

"Relax," the voice continued. "Not going to hurt you. Brianna sent you for the sword."

"You're Mimi." He'd read about her in the files—telepathic, supernaturally long-lived, Brianna's companion for decades. Reading about it and experiencing it were very different things.

"And you're standing on my porch looking nervous. Come inside. There's someone you need to meet."

The cat hopped down and padded toward the door, which swung open on its own. Ross hesitated. Every instinct he'd developed over ten years screamed that walking into a Valensi's home was suicide. But Temper trusted Brianna, and Brianna trusted this arrangement, and right now trust was all any of them had.

He knocked on the doorframe as he stepped inside.

She was standing in the kitchen doorway.

Dark skin, natural hair cropped close to her shoulders, eyes that caught the light wrong—the telltale brightness of a newly turned Valensi. She was gripping the doorframe hard enough to splinter the wood, and her whole body was vibrating with barely contained energy.

"Who the hell are you?"

"Ross. John Sebastian Ross." He kept his hands visible, his posture non-threatening. "Brianna sent me."

"Brianna left me." The words came out raw, ragged. "She left me a note and walked out while I was—" She stopped, swallowed hard. "How do I know you're not here to kill me?"

"If I wanted to kill you, I wouldn't have knocked."

"That's not reassuring."

"It's not meant to be. It's meant to be honest." He took a slow step forward, watching her reaction. She tensed but didn't attack. Good sign. "Brianna is alive. She's working with me and my organization to stop a Valensi named Elijah. She asked me to come here and retrieve a weapon she needs."

"Elijah." The name hit her like a physical blow. "She told me about him. About what he did to her."

"Then you know why she had to leave. Why she couldn't wait for you to wake up."

"She thought she was going to die." Daphne's voice cracked. "She Birthed me because I begged her to, and then she walked out expecting to never come back."

Ross didn't have an answer for that. It was true, and they both knew it.

"She didn't want to do it this way," Mimi's thoughts cut in. The cat had settled on the kitchen counter, watching them both with ancient eyes. "She wanted to be here when you woke. But Elijah forced her hand. He always does."

"You were awake faster than expected," Ross said. "She thought the transformation would take three days."

"It took two." Daphne released the doorframe and looked at her hands—stronger now, steadier, but still unfamiliar. "I woke up an hour ago. Hungry. Scared. Alone." She met his eyes. "Where is she?"

"Preparing. The confrontation happens tonight. 4 AM at Evergreen Cemetery."

"Then I'm going."

"No."

"That wasn't a question." She stepped toward him, and Ross saw the predator lurking beneath the surface. Raw, untrained, but very real. "She's facing this thing alone because of me. Because she thought I'd be unconscious for another day. Well, I'm not. I'm awake, I'm stronger than I've ever been, and I am not letting her die while I sit here waiting."

"You're a fledgling. You've been Valensi for less than two days. You don't know how to fight, how to use your new abilities, how to."

"I've been Valensi for two days. Before that, I was human for thirty-one years." Her jaw set in a way that reminded Ross, uncomfortably, of the stubborn determination he'd seen in soldiers who refused to leave wounded brothers behind. "I've loved that woman for seven years. I waited for her. I watched her push me away, over and over, because she was too scared to let anyone close. And when she finally did. When she finally trusted me enough to give me forever. She walked out the door expecting to die alone."

"Daphne—"

"I don't care if I'm weak. I don't care if I'm untrained. I don't care if I get myself killed." Her eyes were blazing now, bright fire in a face that had been human two days ago. "She is not facing that monster without me. So, either you take me with you, or I find my own way there. But I *am* going."

Ross stared at her. He'd seen a lot of things in his decade of hunting. Monsters and victims, courage and cowardice, every shade of human and inhuman behavior. But he'd never seen anything quite like this. A fledgling Valensi, barely past her transformation, demanding to walk into a fight she couldn't possibly win.

All for love.

"She's serious," Mimi observed. "In case you were wondering."

"I wasn't." Ross sighed. "Fine. You come. But you stay back, you follow my lead, and if I tell you to run, you run. Understood?"

"Understood."

"I mean it. This isn't a negotiation. Elijah is older than anything you can imagine, and he will kill you without a second thought. Your job isn't to fight. It's to survive. To be there for Brianna when this is over."

Daphne's expression shifted. The fierce determination softened into vulnerability.

""You think she'll survive?"

Daphne's expression shifted. The fierce determination softening into something more fragile.

"I think she's survived centuries of hell, and she's not done yet." He moved toward the living room. "Now show me where she keeps the sword."

The living room was clean and organized, just like the rest of the house. The space of someone who valued control, who needed everything in its place. Daphne led him to the fireplace. Ross stood in front of it and took two side steps to the left. He reached down and tapped at the floorboards. One sounded slightly different to the rest.

He shimmied the floorboard lose only to discover the long metallic lockbox. He retrieved the key Brianna had given him. And, within the lockbox...

The sword was beautiful.

Japanese craftsmanship, unbelievably old but perfectly maintained. The blade caught the light with an edge that looked sharp enough to split atoms. Ross lifted it carefully, feeling the balance, the weight of centuries of skill embedded in metal and wood.

"Asaro gave it to her," Daphne said quietly. "About two hundred years ago. He was her teacher, after she became Solari. She told me he was one of the only Valensi who ever treated her like a person instead of a problem."

"She told you a lot."

"She told me everything. Finally." Daphne's voice was thick with emotion. "The night before she left. She told me about Garth, about the mountain, about all the centuries of hiding. She told me about Elijah and what he did in London. She told me why she'd never let anyone close."

"And you still wanted this? Knowing all of that?"

"I wanted her. The rest of it. The pain, the danger, the centuries of carrying grief alone. I wanted to help her carry it." She touched the edge of the lockbox, her fingers tracing patterns only she could see. "That's what love is, isn't it? Showing up, even when it's terrifying."

Ross thought about Rufus. About the night that massive head had settled in his lap, the trust it had represented. About the silence where barking should have been, and the decade of hunting that followed.

"Yeah," he said. "I guess it is."

He sheathed the sword and headed for the stairs.

Three hours later, Brianna stood in a service station restroom and stared at her reflection.

The face looking back was the same one she'd worn for eight centuries. Pale skin, dark hair, features that belonged to a woman in her early forties but held the weight of something far older. She'd looked at this face in a thousand mirrors, in a hundred cities, across generations of human history.

Tonight might be the last time.

She'd sent Ross for the sword hours ago. By now he would have it, would be preparing for the cemetery confrontation. Temper's team would be moving into position. Everything was in place.

Except Daphne.

Brianna closed her eyes and thought about the woman she'd left transforming in her bed. By now the worst of it should be over—the fever breaking, the convulsions fading, the first terrifying moments of consciousness approaching. Daphne would wake up alone. Would find the note, the blood, the instructions. Would realize that Brianna had walked out expecting to die.

Forgive me, she thought. Please. Forgive me.

She opened her eyes and began preparing.

The knife went into a sheath attached to her calf, hidden under her pant leg. Madronite, the weapon Temper had given her. Her clothes were practical: dark, close-fitting, nothing that could be grabbed or used against her. She tied her hair back and checked her range of motion, her balance, her readiness.

Eight hundred years of running. Of hiding, of building walls, of refusing to let anyone close enough to hurt her.

Tonight, she stopped running.

Elijah had taken everything from her once. Had shown her what powerlessness felt like, what it meant to be prey. She'd spent two centuries building herself into something stronger. Solari, daywalker, survivor.

Now it was time to find out if any of it mattered.

She thought about Garth. About the garden in Lyon, the cottage in the mountains, the morning he'd walked out and never returned. Centuries of wondering. Of not knowing.

I never stopped loving you, she thought. I never will. But I can't keep running from the past.

She thought about Daphne. About seven years of patience, of stubborn love, of refusing to give up on someone who was too broken to let herself be saved.

I love you. I should have said it sooner. I should have said it a thousand times.

She thought about Ross. About a Hunter who'd lost his partner and turned his grief into purpose. About the alliance they'd forged, improbable and fragile and absolutely necessary.

Don't miss, she thought. When the moment comes, don't miss.

Brianna looked at her reflection one last time. Then she turned off the light and walked out into the night.

Evergreen Cemetery waited.

21

EVERGREEN

Evergreen Cemetery sprawled across twenty acres of rolling hills and ancient oaks, dotted with weathered headstones that dated back to the Civil War. During the day, it was peaceful. A place where families came to remember, where groundskeepers tended grass and trimmed hedges, where the dead rested quietly beneath Charlotte's suburban sky.

At 3:47 AM, it was something else entirely.

Brianna stood among the oldest graves, where the shadows pooled like black water between the monuments. Across the road, Eastway Middle School sat dark and silent. Daphne's workplace, her daily routine, the life she'd led before Brianna had burned it all down.

The irony wasn't lost on her.

She'd chosen this spot deliberately. Eastern edge, near a massive oak that had been old when Charlotte was young. Room to maneuver, if it came to that. And symbolic enough to draw Elijah exactly where she wanted him.

Somewhere out there, Ross was watching. She didn't know exactly where Temper had positioned him. Didn't want to know, in case Elijah could read it in her face. But knowing he was there, that she wasn't entirely alone in this, helped steady the tremor in her hands.

The night was cold, the kind of December chill that bit through clothing and settled into bones. Brianna didn't feel it. Centuries had taught her to ignore physical discomfort, to push sensation aside and focus on what mattered.

What mattered now was survival.

She heard him before she saw him.

Footsteps on frost-hardened grass. Unhurried. Confident. The walk of someone who had all the time in the world and knew exactly how this encounter would end.

"Brianna."

His voice hadn't changed. Two hundred and twenty-six years, and it still carried the same cultured warmth, the same undertone of amusement that made her skin crawl. She turned slowly, keeping her hands visible, her posture neutral.

Elijah stood twenty feet away, immaculate in a dark suit that certainly cost a pretty penny. His face was the same. Handsome, ageless, with eyes that held centuries of cruelty behind a mask of civility. There was blood on his lips, barely visible in the darkness. He'd fed recently. Good. A sated predator was a careless predator.

"You came," he said. "I confess, I wasn't entirely certain you would."

"You didn't give me much choice."

"There's always a choice, darling. You simply chose the entertaining option." He moved closer, each step deliberate, predatory. "I must say, this location is inspired. The cemetery, the school across the street... you've developed a taste for the dramatic in your old age."

"I learned from the best."

His smile widened. "Flattery. How delightful." He stopped ten feet away, close enough to strike, far enough to give the illusion of safety. "I assume you've had time to reconsider my request?"

"Your demand, you mean."

"Semantics." He waved a hand dismissively. "The Hunter. Where is he?"

"I don't know."

"Lying doesn't suit you, Brianna. It never has." He tilted his head, studying her with those cold, empty eyes. "You visited him in jail. You arranged his release. You've been remarkably busy for someone who claims to know nothing."

"I investigated the case. It's what I do. What I did, before you forced me to resign."

"Forced you?" He laughed. A sound like glass breaking. "I merely suggested you might find the situation worth your attention. Whatever choices you made afterward were entirely your own."

"The way my choices in London were my own?"

The laughter stopped. Cruelty flickered across his face, there and gone in an instant.

"London was a long time ago. I'd hoped you'd moved past it."

"You hoped I'd forgotten." Brianna felt the old rage stirring, the fury she'd buried for two centuries rising toward the surface. "You hoped I'd become so grateful for my continued existence that I'd overlook what you did. What you took."

"What I took?" He stepped closer, and she forced herself not to retreat. "I gave you a gift, Brianna. I showed you what you truly are. Not some romanticized creature of the night, but a predator. A survivor. I stripped away your illusions and let you see the world as it really is."

"You assaulted me. You violated me. You—"

"I taught you." His voice was soft now, almost tender. "Every lesson I gave you made you stronger. The woman you are today. The Solari, the survivor, the creature who walks in daylight while the rest of us sleep. She exists because of what I did. Because of what I showed you was possible."

Brianna's hands were shaking. She clenched them into fists, forcing the tremors to stop.

"You didn't make me Solari. I did that myself. A century of burning, day after day, while you slept in your comfortable darkness. I did that to escape you. To hide somewhere you couldn't follow."

"And yet here we are." He spread his arms, encompassing the cemetery, the night, the impossible situation she'd found herself in. "All roads lead back to me, darling. They always do."

"Not this time."

"No?" He raised an eyebrow. "You're going to stop me? You, alone, outmatched, standing in a graveyard at four in the morning with nothing but righteous indignation and whatever weapon you've hidden under that jacket?"

She drew the Madronite knife from its holster, letting him see the blade. The synthetic wood gleamed dully in the darkness. Not impressive to look at, but deadly to their kind.

His gaze dropped to the weapon. Recognition flickered across his face. "Madronite. The humans have been busy."

"They've had motivation."

"Indeed." He looked back up at her, and the smile returned. Colder now, stripped of pretense. "Very well. If you insist on doing this the hard way..."

He moved.

Fast. Faster than anything Brianna had ever seen. One moment he was standing ten feet away; the next he was in front of her, his hand closing around her throat, lifting her off her feet like she weighed nothing.

"I had such plans for you," he whispered, his face inches from hers. "Centuries of entertainment. A project to occupy my attention during the long, tedious years. But if you're determined to end this prematurely..."

His grip tightened. Stars exploded across her vision.

"...then I suppose we should get started."

He threw her.

She hit a headstone twenty feet away. Ribs cracked. Blood in her mouth. The impact drove the air from her lungs.

Before she could recover, he was there again, his foot coming down toward her wrist. She rolled, came up in a crouch, the Madronite blade still in her grip.

"Interesting." He hadn't even broken stride. "You're faster than I remember."

"I've had two centuries to practice."

"Tell me, darling—who trained you? That wasn't instinct. That was technique."

She didn't answer. Shifted her weight, kept the knife between them.

He came at her. A blur of motion, hands like striking snakes. She blocked, ducked, drove an elbow into his ribs with everything she had.

He grunted. Actually grunted.

Surprise flickered across his features. Then his eyes narrowed.

"That hurt." Something new in his voice. Attention. "That actually hurt."

He came at her differently now. Testing. She blocked a kick, deflected a throat-strike, landed a palm-heel to his chin that snapped his head back.

His hand shot out and caught her wrist. Grip like iron.

"Asaro." A statement, not a question. His grip tightened. "He trained me, you know. Two thousand years ago."

"Then you should know what comes next."

She drove her knee up toward his groin. He twisted, took it on his thigh instead, but the movement gave her the opening she needed. She tore free of his grip and put ten feet between them.

They faced each other across the frozen grass, both breathing harder now. Brianna's ribs screamed with every breath. At least one was cracked, maybe two. But she was still standing. Still fighting.

"I'm impressed," Elijah said. He sounded like he meant it. "You might actually be worth killing properly."

"I'm honored."

"You should be." He rolled his shoulders, cracked his neck. "Then let's see what you've really learned."

He came at her like a storm.

22

BLOOD AND BONE

The next few minutes were the longest of Brianna's existence.

Elijah fought the way a hurricane destroyed. Relentless, overwhelming, impossible to predict. He was everywhere at once, striking from angles that shouldn't have been possible, moving with a speed that made her eight centuries feel like nothing.

Survive. That was the key word. Everything else was secondary.

She blocked a punch that would have caved in her skull. Ducked a kick that whistled past her ear. Landed a strike to his floating ribs that made him hiss.

"Good," Elijah said, almost conversationally. "Very good. You're not just defending. You're looking for opportunities. Asaro taught you well."

He feinted left, came right. She read it, barely, and threw herself backward. His claws raked the air where her face had been.

Claws. He'd extended them at some point during the fight. Long, curved, sharp as surgical steel. This wasn't sparring anymore. This was a killing field.

"You know what I find fascinating about you, Brianna?" He circled her, those terrible claws catching the moonlight. "You actually believe you can win. After everything I've done to you. After London, after the centuries of watching, after everything. You still think this ends with you walking away."

"I think this ends with one of us dead."

"On that, we agree." He lunged.

She couldn't block it. Could only twist so the blow meant for her throat caught her shoulder instead, spinning her around.

He followed up. A throat-chop aimed at ending the fight.

She got her arm up. Blocked.

The impact was like nothing she'd ever felt. She felt the bones in her forearm grind together, felt something in her left hand simply... give way.

The scream tore out of her before she could stop it.

She staggered backward, cradling her hand, and looked down.

Her pinky finger was gone.

Not broken. Not dislocated. Gone. Sheared clean off at the base, leaving nothing but a ragged stump that pumped dark blood onto the frozen grass. Somewhere behind her, she could hear the small wet sound of it landing.

"Oh my," Elijah said. He was looking at his hand, at the blood there, with something like delight. "That wasn't intentional, I assure you."

She attacked.

No technique. No strategy. Eight centuries of control burned away in an instant, leaving nothing but the animal underneath.

The Madronite knife carved through the air, and for one moment, one perfect crystalline moment, she saw fear flicker across Elijah's face.

Then he caught her wrist again.

"Now that," he said, "was almost impressive."

He twisted. The knife fell from her nerveless fingers. Before she could react, his fist connected with her face, and the world went white.

She came back to herself on the ground, tasting blood, her head ringing like a cathedral bell.

Get up. The thought was distant, almost dreamlike. *Get up or he wins.*

She pushed herself up on her good hand. The left one was useless now. The missing finger had stopped bleeding, her body already trying to heal, but the shock of it was still reverberating through her system.

Elijah stood a few feet away, watching her struggle with an expression of mild curiosity.

"You know what I've always admired about you, Brianna? Your stubbornness. Any sensible creature would have surrendered by now. But you..." He shook his head. "You just keep getting up."

"I've had practice."

"Indeed you have." He moved closer. She forced herself to her feet, swaying. "Tell me. Is it pride that keeps you fighting? Or something more personal?"

London. A dark room. His voice in her ear.

She'd spent a century burning herself in the sun to escape him. Had built a new life, a new identity.

And now here they were. Predator and prey.

Except she wasn't prey anymore.

"You made a mistake," she said. Her voice was raw, broken, but steady. "Coming here. Thinking I was still the woman you remember from London."

"Did I?" He raised an eyebrow. "Because from where I'm standing, you look remarkably similar. Bloody. Broken. Struggling to stay on your feet."

"The difference is, I know what you are now." She took a step toward him. Then another. "I've spent two centuries studying you. Learning your patterns. Your weaknesses."

"I don't have weaknesses."

"Everyone has weaknesses." Another step. "Even you. Even the great Elijah, Protector of the Hierarchy, three thousand years of accumulated arrogance in an expensive suit."

His expression shifted. The amusement faded, replaced by something colder. The look of a predator reassessing its prey.

"Careful, darling."

"You know what I figured out, after all those years of watching you? Of studying the patterns?" She was close now. Close enough to see the individual threads in his suit, the ancient cruelty in his eyes. "You hate being reminded of what you used to be."

"And what was that?"

"Human."

The word hung in the air between them.

And Elijah's face changed.

It was subtle, a tightening around the eyes, a tension in the jaw, but Brianna had spent centuries learning to read people, and she saw it clearly. The mask slipping. The ancient wound exposed.

"You were human once," she pressed. "Just like me. Just like all of us. You were born in some village somewhere, lived a human life, had human feelings. And then someone Birthed you, and you spent three thousand years trying to forget that you were ever anything less than a god."

"I was never—"

"You were HUMAN." She spat the word at him. "You crawled in the dirt like the rest of us. You felt fear and pain and weakness. And no matter how many centuries you live, no matter how many people you hurt, you will ALWAYS be the thing you hate most. A creature that used to be human."

He hit her.

Not with technique. Not with the controlled precision of a master warrior. Just raw, explosive rage. A backhand that caught her across the face and sent her spinning.

But she'd been ready for it. Had goaded him into exactly this response.

She rolled with the blow, came up facing him, and saw what she'd been hoping to see: fury. Real, uncontrolled fury. The mask was gone. The sophisticated predator was gone. What remained was something older and uglier. A creature that had been wounded in its deepest place.

"You think you understand me?" His voice was different now. Rougher. The cultured accent was slipping. "You think your pathetic eight centuries give you any insight into what I am? What I've become?"

"I think you're scared." She got to her feet. Slowly, painfully, but she got there. "I think under all that power and cruelty, there's still a frightened little human wondering if any of it matters. If three thousand years of existence have actually meant anything at all."

He came at her like an avalanche.

No strategy. No technique. Just overwhelming force driven by three millennia of rage. His claws raked across her face, and she felt her cheek open up. Not a scratch, not a cut, but a deep, vicious gash that went all the way to the bone.

She screamed.

The pain was indescribable. Fire and ice and broken glass all at once. She could feel the wound pulsing with every beat of her heart, could feel air touching parts of her face that should never feel air. When she gritted her teeth, she could feel the muscles of her cheek pulling against the opening, could taste blood filling her mouth.

He can see my teeth, she realized dimly. *Through my cheek. He can see my back teeth.*

Elijah stood over her, breathing hard, his claws dripping with her blood.

"You want to know what I think?" His voice was barely recognizable now. "I think you're the one who's scared. I think you've always been scared. Of me, of what you are, of what you might become. I think that's why you ran. Why you hid. Why you spent a century burning yourself rather than face the truth."

She couldn't answer. Could barely think through the pain. Her face was a ruin, her hand was missing a finger, her ribs were cracked, and every breath felt like drowning.

"But you know what the real tragedy is?" He crouched down beside her, his face inches from hers. "I was going to let you live. After tonight. I was going to take what I wanted. The Hunter, your little schoolteacher, your pathetic excuse for a life. And then I was going to let you exist. A broken thing, yes. A reminder of what happens to those who defy the Hierarchy. But alive."

He grabbed her by the hair and hauled her upright. The wound in her cheek screamed in protest, fresh blood streaming down her neck.

"Now? Now I think I'll just take my time."

She hung in his grip, barely conscious, the world swimming in and out of focus. Nearly a millennium of existence, and this was how it ended. In a cemetery in Charlotte, at the hands of the monster who had haunted her entire existence.

Daphne, she thought. *I'm sorry. I'm so sorry.*

Then Elijah said something that changed everything.

"You know, I've been saving this. Waiting for the perfect moment." His voice had smoothed out again, regaining its cultured cadence. "A parting gift, you might say. Something to take with you into whatever comes next."

"What..." The word came out slurred, wet with blood. "What are you talking about?"

"Your husband. Garth." He said the name like he was savoring it. "Did you ever find out what happened to him? After all those centuries of searching?"

Ice settled in her chest. Colder than the December air. Colder than the blood loss that was making her vision swim.

"Don't."

"The Hierarchy sent me to deal with both of you, you know. Garth and his unauthorized creation. Both marked for death." Elijah smiled—that terrible, satisfied smile. "But when I found you in that little cottage, so young and so afraid, I saw potential. I convinced my superiors that you might be worth watching. That your suffering might prove... educational."

"What are you saying?"

"I'm saying I was there, Brianna. That autumn evening when your husband left for the village and never came back? I was waiting for him on the road."

The world stopped.

Everything, the cemetery, the pain, the blood, faded into nothing. There was only Elijah's voice, and the truth she'd spent eight centuries searching for.

"He fought well," Elijah continued. "Better than I expected, actually. Your Garth had some skill. But he was young, and I am very, very old." He tilted his head, studying her reaction with obvious pleasure. "It took almost an hour. He kept asking about you, even at the end."

"You—" The word came out as a whisper. "You killed him."

"I killed him." No remorse. No hesitation. "And then I let you live so I could watch. Eight hundred years of watching you search, Brianna. You have no idea how grateful I am."

Something broke inside her then. Not her will. That was already shattered. Not her hope. That had been fading with every blow. Something deeper. Something fundamental.

All those years. All those centuries of wondering. Of searching. Of hoping against hope that somehow, somewhere, Garth was still alive.

And Elijah had known the whole time. Had watched her suffer. Had fed on her grief like it was wine.

"Now," Elijah said, letting her drop to the ground like discarded trash, "I think we're done here. Any last words, darling? Anything you'd like to say before I finish what I started in London?"

Brianna lay in the frozen grass, blood pooling beneath her face, her hand throbbing where her finger used to be, her ribs grinding with every breath.

She should have been finished. Should have been broken beyond repair.

But somewhere in the depths of her shattered soul, something was still burning.

Garth. Her love. Her maker. The man who had given her eternity.

And this monster had taken him from her.

Had taken everything.

"Yes," she whispered. "I have something to say."

Elijah leaned closer, curious despite himself.

"I'm going to kill you." Her voice was barely audible, wet with blood. "I don't know how. I don't know when. But before this night is over, I'm going to watch you die. And I'm going to make sure you know exactly why."

He laughed. Actually laughed. A sound of genuine amusement.

"Oh, Brianna. Even now, even broken and bleeding at my feet, you still think you can—"

He stopped.

Turned toward the cemetery entrance.

And Brianna heard what he heard: footsteps. Running. Getting closer.

Someone was coming.

23

FOR GARTH

Daphne had tried to stay in the car.

She'd promised Ross. Had sat in the passenger seat with her hands clenched in her lap, watching the cemetery through the windshield, listening to the sounds of violence carry across the December air.

But when she heard the scream. That terrible, agonized scream that could only have come from Brianna. Something inside her snapped.

She was out of the car before she knew she was moving.

The cemetery gate was locked. She grabbed the metal and pulled. The lock shattered. The gate flew off its hinges.

Then she was running through the headstones, toward the sounds of pain, toward the woman she loved.

She was not going to let Brianna die alone.

Elijah watched the fledgling come sprinting through the graves with something between amusement and contempt.

Dark skin, amber eyes, moving with the clumsy speed of someone who hadn't yet learned to control their new body. Two days old, maybe three. Still wearing the clothes she'd probably had on when her transformation began.

Pathetic.

"Ah," he said. "The girl."

Daphne skidded to a stop fifteen feet away, her chest heaving, her eyes wild. She was looking at Brianna. At the blood, the wounds, the ruin of her face. And her expression was crumbling.

"Bri?" Her voice was shaking. "Oh God, Bri, what did he—"

"Run." Brianna tried to push herself up and failed. "Daphne, run. You can't—"

"I'm not leaving you."

"How touching." Elijah moved toward the fledgling with lazy confidence. "The cavalry arrives."

"Let her go." Daphne's hands were balled into fists. "Let her go right now."

"Or what? You've been Valensi for two days. You're a child pretending to be a monster."

"I don't care what I am." Daphne took a step forward. "Let. Her. Go."

"Love." Elijah shook his head. "It makes people so wonderfully stupid."

He moved.

One instant he was ten feet from Daphne; the next his hand was around her throat, lifting her off the ground like she weighed nothing. She clawed at his fingers, kicked at his body, but he didn't seem to notice.

"Love," he said, squeezing slightly. Daphne made a choked sound. "It's almost endearing, how you think it matters."

"Let her—" Brianna tried to rise and collapsed. "Elijah, please. This is between us. She's nothing to you."

"She's everything to you. Which makes her infinitely valuable to me."

He turned Daphne to face Brianna, holding her aloft like a trophy. And Daphne saw, really saw, what Elijah had done.

The gash in Brianna's cheek, so deep that bone gleamed white in the moonlight. The mangled left hand, the missing finger leaving a raw, bloody stump. The countless cuts and bruises, the way she lay twisted in the grass like a broken doll. The blood, so much blood, pooling beneath her, soaking into the frozen earth.

Two days ago, Daphne had been human. Two days ago, she'd understood pain and fear and love in human terms.

Now she was something else. Every sensation amplified. Every emotion raw-edged and inescapable. Her body was still adjusting to the Birthing, still flooded with hormones and instincts she didn't understand.

And Brianna. Her Brianna. The woman she'd loved for seven years, the woman who had given her eternity. Lying broken and bleeding in the grass.

The world went gray at the edges. Daphne's body went limp in Elijah's grip, consciousness sliding away like water through her fingers.

The world went gray at the edges. Daphne felt her body going limp in Elijah's grip, felt consciousness sliding away like water through her fingers.

The last thing she heard before the darkness took her was Elijah's voice, cold and dismissive:

"Pathetic. You chose poorly, Brianna. This one is trash."

He threw her aside like a discarded rag, not even bothering to watch where she landed.

Ross had watched the whole thing from behind a marble angel thirty yards away.

Now Brianna lay in the grass, barely moving. Elijah stood over her with the satisfaction of a cat that had cornered its mouse. Daphne was crumpled somewhere behind them, unconscious or worse.

Ross's shoulder was dislocated. Every movement sent fire through his nervous system. His hands were shaking. His vision kept wanting to blur.

But he was still standing. Still holding the sword.

The Japanese blade Brianna had trusted him to retrieve. And the Madronite knife, tucked into his belt. The weapon that could actually kill this monster.

He couldn't kill Elijah himself. But he could create an opening.

This is for Rufus.

He stepped out from behind the angel.

Elijah was focused on Brianna, savoring his victory, monologuing about something. Ross could hear the cultured voice droning on, but couldn't make out the words. The Protector's back was to him. Completely exposed.

Never going to get a better chance than this.

Ross pulled the Madronite knife from his belt.

"BRIANNA!"

He threw the knife. Watched Brianna's head turn, her bloody hand come up, her fingers close around the hilt.

Then Ross charged.

He drove the sword into Elijah's back with every ounce of strength he had left. Felt the blade punch through ancient flesh.

Elijah screamed. Shock more than pain.

He spun, tearing the sword from Ross's grip, his hand finding Ross's throat and lifting him off his feet. The blade was still embedded in his back, unreachable.

"You," Elijah snarled. "You insignificant little—"

"Now."

Elijah turned, still holding Ross, and found her directly in front of him.

She was a ruin. Blood streaming from her face, her hand mangled, barely able to stand. But she was holding the Madronite knife. Her eyes held what had been missing before. Purpose.

"For Garth," she said.

And she drove the blade into his heart.

The effect was immediate.

Elijah released Ross, staggering backward, both hands going to the knife protruding from his chest. His face, that handsome, ageless face, contorted in ways that seemed to defy anatomy.

"What—" He looked down at the blade. "What have you—"

"Madronite." Brianna's voice was hollow, stripped of emotion. "It triggers a cellular reaction in our kind. Spreads through the system. Disintegrates everything it touches."

"No." Elijah tried to pull the knife out, but his hands were shaking, his coordination failing. "No, this isn't—I'm three thousand years old. I've survived—I've survived everything—"

"Not this."

The change started at the wound and spread outward.

His skin began to crack, dark lines spreading like shattered glass. Light, or something like light, leaked from the fissures, cold and terrible. His chest caved inward around the knife, the flesh dissolving, revealing ribs that were already turning to ash.

"You can't." He was backing away now, stumbling over headstones, his body coming apart piece by piece. "The Hierarchy—they'll come for you—they'll destroy everything you've—"

"Let them come."

Brianna followed him. Step by painful step, her body screaming in protest, but she followed. She was going to watch this. She was going to watch every second.

Elijah fell to his knees. His hands were gone now. Crumbling, disintegrating, leaving nothing but ash that scattered in the December wind. His face was next, those ancient eyes finally showing something that looked like fear.

"Brianna." Her name came out distorted, wrong. His jaw was dissolving, his tongue turning to dust. "Please. You don't understand—there's so much more—so much you don't know—"

"I know enough."

She watched him die.

It took a long time. The Madronite spread slowly, methodically, breaking down three millennia of accumulated existence cell by cell. Elijah screamed until his lungs dissolved. He reached for her until his arms turned to dust. He stared at her until his eyes crumbled into nothing.

And then there was only a pile of ash, and a Madronite knife, and the cold December wind.

Ross reached her first.

He was limping, his shoulder hanging at a wrong angle, but he made it to her side before her legs gave out completely. Caught her as she fell, lowered her gently to the frozen grass.

"Is he...?" Ross looked at the pile of ash, at the knife lying in its center.

"Gone." Brianna's voice was barely a whisper. "He's gone."

"The girl, Daphne,"

"Check on her. Please."

Ross nodded, staggering toward where Daphne lay crumpled among the headstones. Brianna watched him go, unable to move, unable to think about anything except the emptiness spreading through her chest.

Three thousand years of existence, reduced to ash in a matter of minutes.

And somehow, it didn't feel like victory.

Daphne was stirring by the time Ross reached her. She sat up slowly, one hand going to her throat, her eyes wild and unfocused.

"Bri? Where's—"

"She's alive." Ross helped her to her feet. "She's alive. It's over."

Daphne pushed past him, stumbling through the headstones toward where Brianna lay. She dropped to her knees beside her, hands hovering over the wounds, afraid to touch, afraid to hurt her more.

"Oh God." Tears were streaming down her face. "Oh God, Bri, your face—your hand—"

"I'll heal." The words came out slurred, wet with blood. "We heal. Remember?"

"You look—" Daphne choked on a sob. "You look like you're dying."

"I've looked worse." It was almost true. "Help me sit up."

Daphne got her arms around Brianna's shoulders, lifted her gently until she was half-sitting, half-leaning against a weathered headstone. The wound in her cheek was still open. Would take hours to heal, maybe days. But the bleeding had slowed. Her hand throbbed where her finger used to be, but that too was already closing over.

She would survive. She always survived.

She just wasn't sure she wanted to.

"He killed Garth." The words came out before she could stop them. "Eight hundred years ago. Elijah killed him. I spent centuries searching, and he was dead the whole time."

Daphne's arms tightened around her. "I heard. Some of it. Bri, I'm so sorry—"

"I should feel something." Brianna stared at the pile of ash, at the knife, at the scattered remains of her tormentor. "He's dead. He's finally dead. I should feel... I don't know. Relief. Victory. Something."

"What do you feel?"

Brianna was quiet for a long moment.

"Empty," she said finally. "I feel empty."

The first light of dawn was beginning to touch the eastern horizon. In a few minutes, the sun would rise over Evergreen Cemetery, illuminating the old headstones and the scattered ash and the three broken people standing in its midst.

Daphne pulled Brianna into her arms and held her tight.

"I'm here," she whispered. "I'm right here. And I'm not going anywhere."

Brianna didn't respond. But after a moment, her arms came up, and she held on like Daphne was the only thing keeping her from falling into the dark.

Ross watched them from a few feet away, the sword still on the ground where it had fallen, his shoulder screaming with every breath.

She should feel something, he thought. *We all should.*

But all he felt was tired. Bone-deep, soul-deep tired. The kind of exhaustion that went beyond physical. That settled into your cells and made you wonder if you'd ever feel anything else again.

The sun broke over the horizon.

The ash that had been Elijah caught the light and glittered briefly before the wind carried it away, scattering three thousand years of cruelty across the cemetery like dust.

The Protector was dead.

And somehow, impossibly, they had survived.

But survival, Brianna was beginning to understand, was not the same as victory.

Victory implied that something had been won.
All she felt was loss.

24

AFTER

Getting home was harder than the fight.

Ross's shoulder was dislocated, possibly broken. Brianna had at least three cracked ribs and a concussion that made the world tilt sideways. Even Daphne, fledgling-strong and mostly unhurt, was shaking too hard to drive steadily.

They made it anyway.

Temper's extraction team found them at the cemetery edge, loaded them into a black SUV, and drove through the brightening streets without asking questions. Professionals. The kind who understood that some nights didn't need debriefing. They just needed ending.

Brianna sat in the back seat, staring out the window at nothing. She hadn't spoken since the cemetery. Hadn't done anything except breathe and blink and let Daphne hold her hand. The emptiness Ross had seen in her eyes was still there. A void where something should have been.

Eight hundred years, he thought. She spent all that time looking for answers.

He understood. When Rufus died, he'd felt something similar. That hollow space where certainty used to live.

The SUV pulled up to Brianna's house. The Hawthorn team helped them inside, did basic first aid, made coffee that no one drank. Then they left, melting back into the morning like they'd never existed.

The three of them sat in Brianna's darkened living room as the sun climbed higher, none of them sure what came next.

The days blurred together.

Brianna slept in fitful stretches, waking with Elijah's name on her lips and Garth's face behind her eyes. Daphne rarely left her side. Bringing blood from the freezer, holding her through the nightmares.

Ross was a different story.

He'd taken the couch that first night, accepting the offered blanket with a grunt that might have been thanks. But sleep didn't come easy. When it came at all.

Daphne woke once in the small hours and found herself standing in the hallway, drawn by a sound she couldn't identify. It took her a moment to realize it was coming from the living room.

Ross was sitting upright on the couch, perfectly still except for his eyes. They swept the room in a continuous circuit—window, door, window, door—the same pattern over and over, like a security camera on an endless loop. His hand rested on his thigh, fingers curved around something that wasn't there.

She must have made a sound, because his head snapped toward her with predator speed. For one terrible instant, his eyes were empty. Not angry. Not afraid. Just... gone. Like the person who lived behind them had stepped out.

Then recognition flickered back. He blinked.

"Go back to sleep," he said. His voice was rust on metal.

"Are you—"

"I'm fine." He turned back to his circuit. Window. Door. Window. Door. "Just keeping watch."

She didn't argue. Didn't point out that the house was warded, that Brianna's security system was supernatural, that there was nothing to watch for anymore.

Some battles, she was learning, didn't end when the enemy died.

Daphne found him at 3 AM on the second night, sitting in the dark kitchen, staring at his hands. They were shaking. A fine tremor that he couldn't seem to stop no matter how hard he pressed them against his thighs.

"Ross?"

He didn't look up. "Go back to bed."

"You're shaking."

"I know." His voice was flat. Dead. "I can't make it stop."

She sat down across from him, keeping distance, reading his body language the way she'd learned to read students who were about to break. "What's happening?"

For a long moment, he didn't answer. Then:

"I keep seeing him."

"Elijah?"

"Rufus." The name came out cracked. "My dog. My partner. The one they killed, ten years ago." His hands curled into fists, still trembling. "I thought I'd dealt with it. Thought I'd turned it into something useful. Purpose, you know? A reason to keep hunting. But now..."

"Now?"

"Now I can't stop seeing his face. The way his neck was broken. The way he looked at me like I was supposed to save him, and I didn't. I wasn't fast enough." Ross finally looked up, and Daphne recognized the look. The hollow stare of someone whose walls had finally crumbled. "I've killed dozens of them since then. Dozens. And it never brought him back. It never made anything better. It just..."

He trailed off, staring at the wall behind her.

"Ross?"

Nothing. He was somewhere else now. Somewhere ten years ago, kneeling in a parking lot covered in ash and blood, watching the sun rise over Charlotte while the only friend he had left lay dead in the building behind him.

Daphne didn't know what to say. Didn't know if there was anything to say. So, she just sat with him in the darkness, keeping vigil over a man who was falling apart.

She was still sitting there an hour later when it happened.

Ross had drifted at some point—not quite sleep, but something close to it. His head had drooped forward, his breathing had slowed. Daphne had been about to slip away, to give him whatever peace he could find, when his whole body went rigid.

His eyes flew open, but they weren't seeing the kitchen. They were seeing somewhere else. Somewhen else.

"No," he breathed. Then, louder: "*No.*"

He was on his feet before she could react, moving with a speed that shouldn't have been possible for someone who'd been half-catatonic seconds ago. He hit the counter with his hip, sent a glass crashing to the floor, didn't seem to notice. His hands were up, reaching for a weapon that wasn't there.

"Rufus! *Rufus, run!*"

Daphne stayed frozen in her chair, afraid that touching him would make it worse. She'd seen this before—not with students, but with her father, in the years after Vietnam. The way the past could reach up and swallow the present whole.

Ross's hands found the edge of the counter and gripped it hard enough to turn his knuckles white. He was panting now, shallow rapid breaths that sounded like they hurt. The tremor was back, worse than before, running through him in waves.

"They're in the building," he said, but he wasn't talking to her. His voice had gone young. Lost. "They're in the building and Rufus is—Rufus is—"

"Ross." She kept her voice low. Gentle. The way she'd learned to talk to her father on the bad nights. "Ross, you're in Charlotte. You're in Brianna's kitchen. The building isn't here. That was years ago."

He didn't respond. His grip on the counter tightened, and she saw a crack appear in the laminate.

"Ross. Feel the counter under your hands. Feel how cold it is. You're not there. You're here. You're safe."

Slowly—so slowly—his breathing began to even out. His eyes blinked, and when they opened again, they were seeing the kitchen. Seeing her. The horror that crossed his face was almost worse than the flashback itself.

"Daphne." His voice cracked. "I—I didn't—"

"It's okay."

"Did I hurt you?"

"No." She stood carefully, moving into his line of sight without crowding him. "You didn't hurt anyone. You just... went somewhere else for a minute."

He looked down at his hands, at the white-knuckled grip on the counter, at the crack he'd left in the surface. When he let go, she could see the indentations his fingers had left.

"I can't stop it," he said. "Every time I close my eyes. Every time I let my guard down. It's right there. Waiting."

"I know."

"You don't." He laughed—a horrible sound, like breaking glass. "You can't. You haven't spent ten years turning yourself into a weapon and then realized the weapon is all that's left. There's nothing underneath anymore. Just... war. Just killing. Just—" He pressed the heels of his hands against his eyes. "God. I can still smell his blood. I can still *feel* it on my hands."

Daphne didn't have an answer for that. So she did the only thing she could think of.

She took a clean dishcloth from the drawer, wet it under the tap, and held it out to him.

"Here," she said quietly. "For your hands."

He stared at it for a long moment. Then his expression crumpled—just for a second, just a flash—and he took the cloth.

He scrubbed at his hands like he was trying to remove skin.

By the third day, Ross had stopped eating.

Daphne tried. She set a plate of scrambled eggs in front of him—the only thing she could make that seemed safe, bland, unlikely to trigger anything. He looked at it like she'd placed a live grenade on the table.

"I'm not hungry."

"You haven't eaten in two days."

"I'm fine."

"You're shaking."

He was. The tremor had spread from his hands to his whole body—a constant low-grade vibration that made him look like he was freezing even in the warmth of the house. He'd lost weight too, she realized. Not much, not yet, but enough that his cheekbones had sharpened, that the hollows under his eyes had deepened into bruises.

"Just try," she said. "One bite."

He picked up the fork like it weighed twenty pounds. Scooped a small amount of egg. Raised it toward his mouth with the concentration of someone defusing a bomb.

The fork stopped an inch from his lips.

For a long moment, nothing happened. Ross just sat there, frozen, the eggs slowly cooling on the tines. Then his jaw tightened. His throat worked. And he set the fork down with exaggerated care, like sudden movements might cause an explosion.

"I can't."

"Ross—"

"I *can't*." His voice broke on the word. "Every time I try to swallow, I taste blood. Copper and ash and—" He shoved back from the table, the chair screeching against the floor. "I'm sorry. I can't."

He retreated to the corner of the living room, folding himself into the space between the bookshelf and the wall. It was a tactical position, Daphne realized. Back to solid surfaces. Clear sightlines to both exits. The kind of place a soldier would choose instinctively.

He sat there for six hours without moving. Just watching. Waiting for an enemy that would never come.

Brianna watched him from the doorway, her own grief temporarily set aside by concern.

"He's breaking down," Mimi observed from her perch on the kitchen counter. "Whatever held him together is coming apart."

"Can you reach him? Telepathically?"

"I tried. His mind is..." The cat paused, searching for words. "Scattered. Like a mirror someone dropped. The pieces are all there, but they don't fit together anymore."

Brianna thought about the cemetery. About Ross approaching Elijah from behind, driving that sword through ancient flesh while knowing it probably wouldn't be enough. About the look on his face when Elijah had him by the throat. Not fear, exactly, but something closer to recognition. Like he'd always known this was how it would end.

"He didn't expect to survive," she said quietly. "None of us did. But he really didn't expect to survive."

"And now he doesn't know what to do with the living."

That evening, while Daphne dozed in the bedroom and Ross stared at the wall in the living room, Brianna slipped out the back door.

She had a meeting to keep.

The diner was a twenty-four-hour place on the edge of uptown. The kind of establishment where nobody asked questions and the coffee was strong enough to strip paint. Brianna slid into a booth near the back and waited.

Temper arrived ten minutes later, looking exactly as he always did: composed, professional, carrying a presence that filled the space without demanding attention. He sat across from her and ordered coffee without looking at the menu.

"You look like hell," he said.

"Accurate."

"How's Ross?"

"Falling apart." Brianna wrapped her hands around her own coffee cup, feeling the warmth seep into her fingers. "He's not handling the aftermath well."

"He never does. Ross is a creature of action. Give him a target and he's unstoppable. Take away the target and he doesn't know what to do with himself." Temper shook his head. "We've been through this before with him. He disappears for a while, sorts himself out, comes back when he's ready."

"And if he doesn't come back?"

"Then we deal with that too." Temper's expression was unreadable. "But that's not why I asked to meet."

"I assumed."

He pulled a folder from his jacket and slid it across the table. "The Hierarchy is in chaos. Word of Elijah's death has spread faster than we expected. Some factions are calling for your head. Others are calling you a hero. The smart ones are waiting to see which way the wind blows."

"And which way is that?"

"Toward war." Temper tapped the folder. "The Magistrate has been building something for decades. An army of Valensi with sun immunity. Solari, like you. He's been recruiting, transforming, training. We don't know the exact numbers, but our intelligence suggests hundreds. Maybe more."

Brianna felt cold settle in her chest. "Thousands?" Temper shrugged nonchalantly.

"They're planning to infiltrate human power structures. Politics, military, finance. Positions where they can shape policy, influence decisions, prepare the ground for..." He spread his hands. "Whatever comes next."

"A takeover."

"Or a war. Or both." Temper leaned forward. "The point is, neutrality isn't an option anymore. The Hierarchy won't forgive what you did, even if some of them secretly applaud it. And the Magistrate views anyone who isn't with him as a threat to be eliminated."

"So, what are you offering?"

"A place. Not as a soldier. We have enough soldiers. As an asset. Someone who can move through Valensi society, gather intelligence, identify threats before they materialize." He met her eyes. "You've spent eight centuries hiding among humans, Brianna. Learning to blend in, to survive, to navigate systems that weren't designed for you. That's a skill set we need."

"You want me to spy on my own kind."

"I want you to help prevent a war that would destroy both our kinds." Temper's voice was quiet, intense. "The Hierarchy won't police itself. We've seen that for centuries. Humans alone can't fight what's coming. But together? With people like you on the inside and organizations like ours providing support?" He shook his head. "That's something different. That's a chance."

Brianna stared at the folder, thinking about everything it represented. A purpose. A direction. A reason to keep moving forward instead of drowning in the emptiness that had swallowed her since the cemetery.

"What about Daphne?"

"What about her?"

"She's newly Birthed. She needs guidance, training, someone to teach her what she's become." Brianna's voice caught. "I can't do that and do what you're asking. Not both. Not well."

"Then find someone who can." Temper's expression softened slightly. "I'm not asking you to abandon her, Brianna. I'm asking you to make a choice about what kind of future you want to build. For her and for everyone else."

Brianna thought about the garden in Lyon, all those centuries ago. About a young woman named Basina who had chosen eternity without understanding what it would cost.

She thought about Garth, dead all along, murdered by the monster she'd finally destroyed.

She thought about Daphne, sleeping in her bed, trusting her, loving her, believing that they'd face whatever came next together.

And she thought about the war that was coming. The war that would sweep away everything if someone didn't stand in its path.

"I need time," she said. "To think. To figure out what this means."

"Take what you need." Temper stood, leaving the folder on the table. "But don't take too long. The world isn't going to wait for any of us to be ready."

He walked out into the night, leaving Brianna alone with cold coffee and impossible choices.

25

PARIS

The next evening, Brianna came home to find a stranger on her porch.

She'd spent the day thinking. Walking through Charlotte's parks, sitting in coffee shops, turning Temper's offer over in her mind until the edges were worn smooth. By the time she pulled into her driveway, the sun was down and her thoughts were no clearer than they'd been that morning.

Then she saw her.

A young woman, or something that looked like a young woman, sat on the porch swing, one leg tucked beneath her, watching the sunset with an expression of profound exhaustion. She had unnaturally red-dyed hair and she sat with the particular stillness of someone who'd learned that movement attracted attention.

Mimi was curled in her lap, purring.

That was what stopped Brianna from reaching for a weapon. Mimi didn't curl up with strangers. Mimi barely curled up with people she'd known for decades.

"She's nice," Mimi's voice whispered in her mind as Brianna approached. "Sad, but nice. She's been waiting for hours. Very patient."

The stranger looked up as Brianna climbed the porch steps. Her eyes were old, centuries old at least, and they held a weight that Brianna recognized. The weight of someone who'd lost everything and was still trying to figure out how to keep breathing.

"Brianna Van Demir," the stranger said. It wasn't a question.

"Yes. And you are?"

"Paris." She didn't offer a last name. Perhaps she didn't have one anymore. "I've come a long way to find you."

They sat in the living room. Brianna in her usual chair, Paris on the couch, Mimi maintaining her position in the stranger's lap like a furry seal of approval. Daphne had emerged from the bedroom at the sound of voices and now hovered in the doorway, uncertain whether to join or retreat.

"How did you find me?" Brianna asked.

"I've been following my own path for weeks. When I heard he was hunting in Charlotte, hunting a Valensi who'd caught his attention, I knew I had to come." Paris stroked Mimi's fur absently, her gaze distant. "He and I have history. The kind you don't forget."

"Had," Brianna corrected. "He's dead."

Relief flickered across Paris's face, mixed with surprise. "You killed him?"

"With help." Brianna nodded toward the living room, where Ross should have been sitting. But his corner was empty. He must have retreated to another part of the house when the stranger arrived. "A Hunter. And Daphne."

Paris's gaze moved to the doorway, taking in Daphne with an assessing look. "You're newly made. I can smell it on you."

"A little while ago, yes," Daphne said, stepping into the room. "Brianna Birthed me."

"Before the battle with Elijah?"

"During. More or less." Daphne settled on the arm of Brianna's chair, close enough to touch. "It's been a complicated couple of weeks."

Paris laughed. A short, surprised sound, like she'd forgotten she was capable of it. "I imagine so." She turned back to Brianna. "I should explain why I'm here."

"Please."

"I'm an exile." The word came out flat, matter-of-fact. "Two weeks ago, I killed a member of the High Guard in Paris. The Magistrate has ordered my death. I've been running ever since. Down to Florida, back up through Georgia and South Carolina, following rumors and hoping to find..." She trailed off, shaking her head. "I don't know what I was hoping to find. Somewhere safe, maybe. Someone who understood."

"You killed her?" Brianna's voice held a touch of dismay. This Paris was a former High Guard. What she was describing seemed...unfeasible.

"That wasn't the plan."

"I should think not. Why?"

"Because she was going to kill someone I cared about. A friend who had..." Paris paused, choosing her words carefully. "Made choices the Hierarchy didn't approve of. I had a split second to decide: my duty or her life." Her jaw tightened. "I chose her life. And everything I'd built for a hundred and thirty-five years burned down in that moment."

Brianna thought about her own choices. The ones that had led her here, to this moment, with a dead Protector behind her and an impossible decision ahead.

"Where is your friend now?"

"I don't know. She disappeared into the night after I saved her. I hope she made it somewhere safe, but..." Paris shrugged, a gesture that couldn't quite hide the grief beneath it. "I may never know."

"And the person you loved? You mentioned someone..."

Paris's expression closed like a door slamming shut. "He thinks I'm dead. It's better that way. Safer for him."

The room fell silent. Mimi continued purring, a soft counterpoint to the weight of unspoken pain.

"You came here looking for what?" Brianna finally asked. "Shelter? Allies?"

"I came here looking for a reason to keep going." Paris met her eyes. "I've spent two weeks running, hiding, trying to figure out what comes next. And everywhere I went, I heard stories. About a Valensi in Charlotte who'd caught Elijah's attention. About a Valensi who played attorney and kept a telepathic cat. About someone who'd been hiding for centuries, just like me." She spread her hands. "I thought maybe—if you'd figured out how to survive this long. You might know something I don't."

"I don't have answers, Paris. I barely have questions anymore."

"Then maybe we can figure them out together." Paris glanced at Daphne, then back at Brianna. "I'm not asking for charity. I'm asking for... I don't know. A place to rest. A chance to catch my breath before the world catches up with me again."

Brianna looked at this stranger. This exile, this fugitive, this woman who'd thrown away everything for a friend who might already be dead. She saw herself, in a way. Saw all the choices she'd made over eight centuries, all the times she'd run, all the walls she'd built.

"You can stay," she said. "For now. We'll figure out the rest as we go."

Paris's shoulders dropped. A release of tension she'd probably been carrying since the moment she'd killed that Guard. "Thank you."

"Don't thank me yet. Things are... complicated. There's a war coming. Forces moving that I'm only beginning to understand." Brianna stood. "But for tonight, you're safe here. That's the best I can offer."

"That's more than I've had in weeks."

Daphne spoke up from her perch on the chair arm. "Have you eaten? We have blood in the freezer. Salmon, mostly. It's not exactly gourmet, but..."

"Salmon blood?" Paris blinked. "You're Solari?"

"I am," Brianna said. "It's a long story."

"I'd like to hear it. If you're willing to tell it."

Brianna considered the request. Considered this stranger who'd appeared on her porch like an answer to a question she hadn't asked yet.

"Tomorrow," she said. "Tonight, rest. Tomorrow, we talk."

They talked for three days.

Paris shared her story. The broad strokes of it, at least. The exile, the flight, the friend she'd saved and the lover she'd lost. She spoke about the Magistrate and his plans, about the High Guard and the Hierarchy, about the war that was brewing between Valensi and humans.

Brianna shared pieces of her own history in return. Not everything, some wounds were too raw especially now, but enough. The garden in Lyon. The centuries of hiding. London, and what Elijah had done there. The decision to become Solari.

Daphne listened, asked questions, tried to make sense of a world that had only existed for her for two weeks. She was learning—absorbing information with the desperate hunger of someone who knew her survival depended on understanding things she'd never imagined.

Ross remained a ghost. He appeared occasionally. Getting water, using the bathroom. He had joined them for Paris' tale. Never spoke beyond monosyllables. The tremor in his hands had gotten worse, and Brianna sometimes heard him pacing in the small hours of the morning, walking circuits through the house like a caged animal.

"He's disappearing," Paris observed on the third night, after they'd heard his footsteps pass the living room for the dozenth time. "I've seen it before. Soldiers who've seen too much. The mind can only hold so much horror before it starts shutting down."

"Will he come back?"

"Some do. Some don't." Paris's expression was sympathetic but unsentimental. "You can't save someone who doesn't want to be saved. You can only be there when they're ready to try."

That night, Brianna sat alone on the back porch, watching the stars wheel overhead. She thought about Ross, falling apart in her living room. About Paris, searching for meaning in a world that had cast her out. About Daphne, newly born into a life she barely understood.

And she thought about Temper's offer. The folder still sat on her kitchen table, unopened since she'd brought it home. A purpose. A direction. A chance to do something that mattered.

But it would mean leaving. It would mean choosing the fight over the people she loved.

Mimi padded out onto the porch and settled beside her.

"You've already decided," the cat observed. "You just haven't admitted it to yourself yet."

"Have I?"

"You're Brianna Van Demir. You've spent almost a thousand years surviving, hiding, protecting yourself. And now you have a chance to do more than survive." Mimi's eyes gleamed in the darkness. "You were never going to say no."

Brianna closed her eyes. The cat was right. She'd known since the moment Temper had made his offer. Maybe since before that—since the moment she'd plunged that knife into Elijah's chest and felt nothing but empty.

"Daphne won't understand."

"Daphne loves you. Understanding will come later." Mimi stood, stretched, began padding back toward the door. "Paris is here for a reason. The universe doesn't make that kind of coincidence. Perhaps she's the answer you've been looking for."

The door closed behind the cat, leaving Brianna alone with the stars and the terrible clarity of what she was about to do.

26

DECISIONS

She stayed on the porch long after Mimi had gone.

The stars were the same stars. That was the thing about stars—they outlasted everything she'd loved and lost, continued their indifferent circuits, gave nothing back. She knew them by the names Garth had taught her: the Latin, the Greek, the farmers' names used for planting. He'd pressed them on her like a gift, patient in the way of someone who understood that most gifts are only understood later.

She had forgotten most of the names.

She thought he would have found that funny.

After a time, she stood.

Inside, the house was quiet. The hall light burned at its usual low setting. She passed Paris's closed door—no sound from within—and the bathroom, and the living room where Ross had folded his blanket with military precision before leaving. She'd heard him go around midnight: the careful click of the latch, the particular silence of a person trying not to take up space in the world. She had not stopped him. She understood that kind of leaving. Some departures weren't about the people left behind.

She stopped at the end of the hall.

Daphne's door was ajar. A sliver of lamplight fell across the floorboards.

Brianna pushed it open.

Daphne was asleep on her side, one hand tucked beneath her cheek, a book closed beside her with a library bookmark tilting precariously from the pages. Her face in sleep had shed the careful composure she maintained during the day—the effort of cataloguing a world that had grown louder and stranger since her Birthing, every sensation arriving at a volume she hadn't chosen. Asleep, she was simply herself. The woman who had waited seven years for Brianna to open a door that Brianna had kept locked since Lyon.

Brianna leaned against the doorframe and looked at her friend...and, lover.

She had been furious at Garth for eight hundred years.

She had called it grief, because fury required a target and grief required only an absence. She had made a wall of it. The slow, patient construction of eight centuries. And, she told herself it was wisdom. Told herself she was simply someone who had learned not to hold on.

She had not known, until two nights ago, that he hadn't left.

She had not known that Elijah had taken him. That there had been no choice, no morning when Garth had considered the cost and walked away. Only a man dragged out of the world before he could say goodbye. Only eight hundred years of her own anger aimed at the wrong absence.

She looked at Daphne sleeping.

He would have left anyway, she thought. The understanding arrived without bitterness, just recognition, the specific clarity of something finally understood after a very long time. If Garth had seen what was coming. If he had known what staying would require her to witness. He would have walked out of that room in Lyon and let her hate him for it, because hating him was survivable in a way that watching him be destroyed was not. He would have made himself the villain of her story rather than subject her to the alternative.

She knew this about Garth because she knew this about herself.

Daphne's chest rose and fell. Her brow was smooth.

Temper had asked what kind of future she wanted to build. For Daphne and for everyone else. The answer had been forming since before he'd framed the question—perhaps since the moment she'd driven the knife into Elijah's chest and felt, beneath the exhaustion and the grief, something that wasn't emptiness after all. Something that wanted to be used.

She was not leaving because the mission was more important than Daphne. She had spent eight centuries constructing versions of that argument and none of them had ever been true. Love was not a lesser thing. It was precisely the thing. It was the reason the rest of it mattered at all.

She was leaving because Daphne deserved a world that was worth living in for three hundred years. For five hundred. Because someone had to stand between what was coming and the people she loved, and she was Solari, she was eight hundred and seventy years old, she had been surviving impossible situations since before Charlotte was a city. She was the right person for this work. And she was the wrong person to stay.

Garth had made her that way. Given her the sun and the centuries and the particular stubbornness of someone who had learned to survive everything.

She was finally going to use it the way he would have wanted.

She drew the door closed until only the sliver of lamplight remained.

Paris was the right choice. She had arrived at Brianna's door like an answer to a question Brianna hadn't known she was asking—exiled, hunted, still moving. Someone who had thrown away everything for a friend and kept going. Someone who understood what it meant to carry grief as luggage rather than armor.

Daphne would not be abandoned. She would be placed in the care of someone who knew what it was to start over with nothing, and who would not flinch at the work of it.

It was not the same as staying. Nothing would ever be the same as staying.

But it was the best she could give.

In the kitchen, she found the notepad she kept by the phone.

She sat down. For a long time, she held the pen without writing.

There was no sentence equal to this. No construction that made eight centuries of earned knowledge into something a woman two weeks Valensi could receive without breaking under. She would write something inadequate, and it would be read by someone who deserved better. She was going to do it anyway, because the alternative was silence, and silence was what cowards left.

She wrote:

She is all I have. She is all I love.
Please take her, teach her, protect her.

She read it back. It was not enough. It would have to be enough.

She folded the paper in half and wrote Paris on the front in her careful, old-fashioned hand—the hand Garth had watched form over three years of Lyon winters, back when her letters still had the shapes of a French girl's education.

She left it on the kitchen table where it would be found.

She did not go back down the hall. She had said goodbye already, in the only way that was possible: by looking, and remembering, and choosing this anyway.

She went to find her coat.

27

DEPARTURES

Ross was gone.

Daphne discovered it first, on the morning of the fourth day. She'd gone to check on him. A habit she'd developed over the past few days, making sure he was still breathing, still present, still fighting whatever battle raged behind his hollow eyes.

But the couch was empty. The blanket was folded neatly on the cushion. And every trace of John Sebastian Ross had vanished from Brianna's house.

No note. No explanation. No goodbye.

Just absence where a person used to be.

"He does this," Brianna said, when Daphne reported the discovery. Her voice was flat, unsurprised. "Temper told me. When things get too heavy, he disappears. Finds somewhere to fall apart in private."

"Shouldn't we look for him?"

"He doesn't want to be found. That's the point." Brianna stared out the kitchen window, her coffee growing cold in her hands. "He'll come back when he's ready. Or he won't. Either way, it's his choice to make."

Daphne wanted to argue. Wanted to say that you didn't just abandon people who were drowning, that you reached out even when they pulled away. But something in Brianna's expression stopped her—a distance that hadn't been there before, a coldness that felt like preparation.

"Are you okay?" she asked instead.

"I'm fine."

It was a lie. They both knew it was a lie. But Daphne didn't push. She'd learned, over seven years of loving this woman, that pushing only made her retreat further.

Paris found them in the kitchen an hour later, reading the silence with the instincts of someone who'd survived by paying attention to the things people didn't say.

"Something's wrong."

"Ross left," Daphne said. "Sometime during the night."

"I'm not surprised." Paris poured herself a cup of coffee from the pot on the counter. "He was held together with string and spite. Once the battle ended, he didn't have anything left to fight."

"Will he be okay?"

"Define okay." Paris sat at the kitchen table, cradling her cup. "He'll survive. Men like that always do. But okay?" She shook her head. "Some people don't come back from the places they go."

Brianna said nothing. She finished her coffee, rinsed the cup in the sink, and excused herself to shower. The mechanical precision of her movements made Daphne's chest ache.

Something was wrong. Something beyond Ross, beyond Elijah, beyond the obvious trauma they were all carrying.

She just couldn't figure out what.

The next morning, Brianna was gone too.

Daphne woke to an empty bed. Not unusual; Brianna often rose before dawn. But the house felt different. Quieter. Smaller. Like something essential had been removed.

She found Paris in the living room, sitting on the couch with a piece of paper in her hands. The older Valensi's face was carefully blank, but her eyes held quiet sorrow.

"What is that?"

Paris looked up. "She left a note."

"What?" Daphne crossed the room in three strides, reaching for the paper. "Let me see."

"Daphne—"

"Let me see."

Paris handed it over.

The handwriting was Brianna's. Elegant, old-fashioned, the penmanship of someone who'd learned to write when calligraphy was still considered essential. The note was short. Too short for what it was trying to say.

Paris—

She is all I have. She is all I love. Please take her, teach her, protect her.

San Diego has a wonderful supernatural community. Safety. Go see Rahne. Tell her I sent you.

We will meet again.

-B

Daphne read it three times. The words didn't change. They just kept sitting there, black ink on white paper, destroying everything she'd thought she understood.

"No." The word came out cracked, broken. "No, this isn't—she wouldn't—"

"Daphne—"

"She wouldn't leave me." Daphne looked up, and the tears were already falling. "Not after everything. Not after what we—she chose me. She Birthed me. She said—"

Her voice gave out. The note fell from her fingers, drifting to the floor like a dead leaf.

Paris didn't try to catch it. Didn't try to offer comfort. She just sat there, watching, with the patience of someone who'd seen this kind of grief before.

"She left," Daphne whispered. "She actually left."

"Yes."

"Without saying goodbye. Without explaining. Without—" A sob tore through her chest. "I would have gone with her. Wherever she's going, whatever she's doing, I would have followed her anywhere. Didn't she know that?"

"I think that's why she didn't ask."

The words hit like a blade. Daphne stared at Paris, trying to make sense of them.

"What?"

"Whatever Brianna's doing, wherever she's going. She didn't want you there. Not because she doesn't love you." Paris's voice was gentle now, almost maternal. "Because she does. Because she's trying to protect you the only way she knows how."

"By abandoning me?"

"By giving you a chance to become something other than her shadow."

Daphne wanted to scream. Wanted to tear the house apart, run into the street, hunt Brianna down and demand answers. But her legs wouldn't move. Her voice wouldn't work. All she could do was stand there, crying, while the world she'd thought she understood crumbled around her.

"She's gone," she said again. "They're both gone."

"Yes." Paris stood slowly, crossing to where Daphne stood frozen. "They made their choices. Now you have to make yours."

"What choice? There's nothing left."

"There's San Diego. There's Rahne, whoever that is. There's me." Paris put a hand on Daphne's shoulder. Gentle, grounding. "I know this hurts. I know it feels like dying. But you're not dead, Daphne. You're just lost. And lost isn't the same as finished."

Daphne looked at this stranger. This exile, this fugitive who'd arrived on the porch three days ago looking for a reason to keep going.

She didn't know her. Didn't trust her. Didn't have any reason to believe that Paris was anything other than another person who would leave.

But she was here. Right now, in this moment, she was the only one who hadn't disappeared.

"I can't—" Daphne's voice broke. "I don't know how to do this."

"I know." Paris pulled her into an embrace. Awkward at first, then tighter as Daphne collapsed against her. "I know. But you don't have to figure it out alone."

They stood like that for a long time. Two broken women holding each other up while the sun rose over Charlotte and the world kept turning without them.

The days that followed were the hardest of Daphne's life.

She couldn't eat. Couldn't sleep. Couldn't stop reading that note, those inadequate words that were supposed to explain why the woman she loved had walked away.

She is all I have. She is all I love.

Then why? Why leave? Why not take her along, wherever she was going? Why make this choice for both of them?

Paris stayed. That was the one constant in a world that seemed determined to fall apart. She didn't push. Didn't offer platitudes. She just... remained. Making meals that Daphne didn't eat. Sitting in silence during the long nights. Holding her when the grief became too much to bear alone.

"I've seen this before," Paris said one evening, after a particularly brutal crying jag had left Daphne hollow and exhausted. "This kind of pain."

"Have you?"

"I left someone too. Someone I loved more than anything." Paris's eyes were distant, seeing something that wasn't there. "I made myself dead to him. Let him believe I was gone forever. Because I thought it was the only way to keep him safe."

"Did it work?"

"I don't know. I'll probably never know." She looked at Daphne. "But I know this: the leaving wasn't about not loving him. It was about loving him too much to watch him die because of me."

"You think that's what Brianna did?"

"I think Brianna has spent eight centuries learning that love is dangerous. That everyone she cares about ends up hurt, or dead, or lost. And I think when she finally let herself love you, really love you, it terrified her more than Elijah ever did."

Daphne thought about the past weeks. The Birthing. The battle. The way Brianna had looked at her afterward, with that terrible emptiness in her eyes.

"She was always going to leave," she realized. "Wasn't she?"

"I don't know. Maybe she thought she could stay. Maybe she wanted to." Paris shook her head. "But wanting and doing aren't the same thing. And some people are better at running than staying."

"I hate her."

"No you don't."

"I want to hate her."

"That's different." Paris reached over and squeezed her hand. "Hate would be easier. But you love her. You'll always love her. The question is whether you can build a life around that love instead of being destroyed by it."

Daphne didn't have an answer. She wasn't sure there was one.

But for the first time since finding that note, she felt something other than grief.

It might have been hope.

Or maybe it was just the stubborn refusal to let this be the end of her story.

28

WESTWARD

A week after Brianna left, Paris started pushing.

Gently, at first. Small things. Opening the curtains to let in the evening light, setting a cup of warmed blood in front of Daphne without being asked, sitting beside her on the couch instead of across the room.

"You can't stay here forever," she said one night.

Daphne was curled in Brianna's chair. The one she'd claimed as her own in those first weeks of learning what forever meant. It still smelled like her. Sometimes Daphne thought that was the only thing keeping her tethered to reality.

"Why not?"

"Because this house isn't yours. Because the Hierarchy may come looking for whoever killed their Protector. Because." Paris paused, choosing her words carefully. "Because you're rotting, Daphne. I can see it happening. And I'm not going to sit here and watch."

"What do you care?"

"I don't know yet." Paris sat on the arm of the couch, close but not too close. "But Brianna asked me to protect you. To teach you. And I can't do that if you're determined to wither away in a dead woman's chair."

"She's not dead."

"You know what I mean."

Daphne did know. That was the problem. Brianna might as well be dead, for all the good it did. She was gone. Vanished into whatever purpose had called her away. And she'd made it clear that Daphne wasn't invited to follow.

"San Diego," she said finally. "The note said San Diego."

"Rahne. Someone Brianna knows, apparently. Someone with connections to the supernatural community out west." Paris shrugged. "I don't know anything about them. But it's a destination. A direction. Better than staying here and waiting for the walls to close in."

"You'd come with me?"

"I'd take you. That's what Brianna asked." Paris met her eyes. "But it's not just about fulfilling a request from someone I barely know. I've been where you are, Daphne. Lost. Grieving. Certain that nothing would ever feel right again. And I know, I know, that the only way through is forward."

Daphne thought about the past seven years. The waiting. The hoping. The slow erosion of her patience and her pride as she'd loved a woman who refused to love her back.

And then, finally, Brianna had let her in. Had given her everything. Eternity, truth, herself. For one brief, perfect moment, Daphne had been happy.

Now she was alone again. But this time, she wasn't human. She couldn't go back to the life she'd had before. Couldn't return to teaching middle school, to grading papers and attending faculty meetings and pretending to be normal.

The only way out was through.

"Okay," she said. "San Diego. Let's do it."

They left three days later.

Paris had acquired a car, Daphne didn't ask how, and they loaded it with the few things that mattered: clothes, Brianna's blood stores, Mimi.

The cat had opinions about the road trip.

"I'm too old for this," she complained telepathically as Paris settled her in a carrier in the back seat. "Sixty-three years of comfortable living, and now I'm being hauled across the country like luggage."

"You could stay," Daphne offered.

"And let you two idiots wander into the desert without supervision? I don't think so." Mimi curled into a ball, her tail twitching with displeasure. "Someone has to keep you alive until you learn to do it yourselves."

They pulled out of Charlotte as the sun set, heading west on I-85. The city lights faded behind them, replaced by the deeper darkness of rural North Carolina. Paris drove; Daphne sat in the passenger seat and watched the mile markers tick past.

"Tell me about yourself," Paris said, somewhere around Gastonia. "Not the Valensi stuff. That's too new. Tell me about who you were before."

"Before Brianna?"

"Before any of it. Who was Daphne Jenkins when she was just... Daphne Jenkins?"

It was a strange question. Daphne hadn't thought about that person in weeks. The human woman who'd taught seventh-grade social studies and collected vintage cameras and spent her weekends hiking in the Blue Ridge Mountains. That woman felt like a stranger now. A character in a story she'd once read.

But Paris was asking. And they had a long drive ahead.

"I grew up in Asheville," Daphne said. "Only child. Parents divorced when I was twelve. I was the quiet kid. Always reading, always watching, never quite fitting in."

"What did you read?"

"Everything. History, mostly. I was obsessed with the idea that the world was bigger than what we could see. That there were secrets hidden underneath the surface of things." She laughed. A rusty sound, but real. "Turns out I was right about that."

"How did you meet Brianna?"

"The library over at UNCC campus. I was there for a book on French poetry. Apparently, she was, too." Daphne shook her head. "I don't know how to explain it. It was like seeing someone you've known your whole life, except you've never met them before. Like recognition."

"Love at first sight?"

"More like terror at first sight. She was so beautiful, so composed, so completely out of my league. When we laughed about reaching for the same book... Her laugh. God. How I miss her laugh." Daphne smiled at the memory. "When we chatted, she looked at me like I was a puzzle she couldn't quite solve. I think that's what made her curious enough to say yes to coffee."

"And then seven years of waiting."

"Seven years of waiting. Seven years of being pushed away and pulled back, of almost-moments and near-misses and the constant feeling that I was loving someone who'd already decided she couldn't be loved." Daphne's voice caught. "I should have walked away. A hundred times, I should have walked away. But I couldn't. She was..." She trailed off, unable to find words big enough.

"She was worth it," Paris finished.

"Yes. Even now. Even after this." Daphne wiped her eyes. "She's still worth it."

They drove in silence for a while. The road unspooled before them, an endless ribbon of asphalt cutting through the darkness.

"I had someone like that," Paris said eventually. "Garrett. I loved him more than anything I'd ever loved. And I had to let him go—let him think I was dead. To keep him safe."

"Do you regret it?"

"Every day. Every single day since I walked away." Paris's hands tightened on the wheel. "But I also know that if I'd stayed, he'd be dead now. The Magistrate would have used him to get to me. Would have destroyed him just to watch me break."

"How do you live with that?"

"You just do. You wake up, and you breathe, and you find reasons to keep going. The reasons change over time. But as long as you have them, you survive."

Daphne considered this. "What's your reason now?"

Paris glanced at her. A quick look, weighted with something Daphne couldn't quite name.

"Right now? You are."

The days blurred together.

They drove through Georgia and Alabama, through Mississippi and Louisiana, through the endless flatness of Texas. They talked—about everything and nothing, about the past and the future, about the world they'd left behind and the one waiting ahead.

Paris told stories about her century of existence. The places she'd been, the people she'd known, the mistakes she'd made and the lessons she'd learned from them. She spoke about the Magistrate and the Hierarchy, about the war that was coming and the impossible choices that lay ahead.

Daphne listened. Absorbed. Began to understand the scope of what she'd become. Not just a Valensi, but a player in a game that had been running for millennia.

And slowly, imperceptibly, she began to heal.

It wasn't forgiveness. Not yet, maybe not ever. The wound Brianna had left was too deep for that. But it was... acceptance. Recognition that the world kept turning whether you were ready for it or not.

"You're stronger than you know," Paris told her one night, somewhere in New Mexico. They'd stopped at a rest area, sitting on a picnic table and watching the stars wheel overhead. "I've seen a lot of fledglings break under less than what you're carrying. But you're still here. Still fighting."

"I don't feel like I'm fighting. I feel like I'm just... existing."

"Sometimes that's the same thing." Paris nudged her shoulder. "Survival isn't always dramatic. Sometimes it's just showing up for another day."

Daphne thought about that as they drove the final stretch into California. About survival and strength and the slow, painful process of becoming someone new.

She wasn't the woman who'd walked into that library seven years ago. She wasn't even the woman who'd woken up in Brianna's house two weeks ago, transformed and terrified and desperately in love.

She was something else now. Someone else. And she didn't know yet who that person would become.

But she was going to find out.

They crested the final hill at midnight.

San Diego spread out before them like a constellation fallen to earth. A million lights glittering against the darkness of the Pacific, stretching from the mountains to the sea. It was beautiful in a way that made Daphne's chest ache.

"There it is," Paris said, slowing the car. "The shining jewel in the desert."

Daphne stared at the city below. Somewhere down there was Rahne, whoever that was. Somewhere down there was a supernatural community, a safe haven, a new beginning.

Somewhere down there was the next chapter of her story.

"Are you ready?" Paris asked.

Daphne thought about Brianna. Wherever she was, whatever she was doing. Thought about the note that sat folded in her pocket, worn soft from handling: She is all I have. She is all I love.

"No," she said honestly. "But I don't think ready matters anymore."

Paris smiled. The first real smile Daphne had seen from her since Charlotte. "It never does."

She put the car in gear, and they began the descent toward the lights.

Behind them, the desert stretched dark and silent, keeping its secrets.

Ahead, San Diego waited to reveal its own.

A MOMENT

If Brianna's story resonated with you, a review helps other readers find their way here. Every one matters more than you might think.

Thank you for reading.

STAY IN THE SHADOWS

Join the Studio Valensi mailing list for release dates, exclusive short fiction from the world of the Valensi, and the occasional dispatch from the darkness.

www.CLStegall.com/subscribe

Your email stays as secret as the Citadel.

ABOUT THE AUTHOR

C.L. Stegall spent a decade in U.S. Army Military Intelligence, a career that bestowed two gifts essential to fiction writing: an appreciation for secrets worth keeping and a finely honed ability to make things up convincingly. After ten years of service, he traded one set of classified documents for another—manuscripts—and hasn't looked back.

Now working under the Studio Valensi banner, CL writes across modern fantasy, contemporary thrillers, and horror, often blending genres in ways that keep readers guessing and slightly unsettled. His work explores the strange territories where myth bleeds into the mundane, where monsters wear familiar faces, and where the supernatural has paperwork and office politics just like everyone else.

Before fully committing to the writing life, CL served as President and Senior Editor at Dark Red Press, sharpening an editorial eye that now torments his own drafts through countless revisions. Because one creative pursuit is never quite enough, Studio Valensi also serves as home for original music demos—soundtracks for stories that don't exist yet and a few that do.

CL lives in Plano, Texas, with his wife Mona and a black cat named Shoyu who has never offered a single note on any manuscript but maintains an air of devastating literary judgment, nonetheless.

When not writing, CL is likely deep in a research rabbit hole about mythology, obscure history, or something unsettling enough that his browser history could raise eyebrows. He maintains that all of it is "for a book," and this is technically true at least sixty percent of the time.

ACKNOWLEDGMENTS

It's rare that a novel is ever the work of one single person. We need eyes on. We need feedback to see if what we are trying to accomplish even makes sense.

Luckily, I've had an insane amount of luck for years with those who really connected with my characters in this tale.

This is set of novels is a trilogy, and the story has grown to unbelievable portions given the wonderful conversations I've had with so many people. Too many to name.

However, I would like to call out all my Army buddies from Panama who read the initial tale back in the early 90s. (Oh, my!)

Also, my lovely, irrepressible Wife, Mona, has been my sounding board for almost 30 years. Love you, babe!

Thank you, sincerely, to all who've had a hand in shaping Paris' story.

I hope you really love what plays out and how it plays out.

This is for you all!